THIEVES BERTH

C. S. STEIN

THIEVES BERTH

Jeweled Sea Press

Jeweled Sea Press

CONTENTS

INTRODUCTION

A number of years ago Carolyn arrived home after a trip to find that our new house had been burgled. Not once. Not twice. But multiple times over the course of a few weeks. The burglars were thorough and malicious. They dumped out our flour on the kitchen floor to find out if we were hiding diamonds. (We weren't.) They spoiled our religious items. They pooped on our floor.

Aside from the emotional trauma and violation, it was a devastating loss that took tens of thousands of dollars to repair and replace items. With that in our past you might think that we would have no truck with thieves.

But no. We're not sure what it is, but we're attracted to fictional thieves. There's just something about sneaking into other people's houses or museums or other places to find out what they have and then figuring out a way to take it that we find fascinating. Besides, when was the last time you heard about a murderer with a heart of gold? Never. Right?

But thieves? The fictional worlds of thieves teem with Robin Hoods.

Being on the wrong end of a theft is horrible, especially when the insurance company takes three months to help you get back on your feet. But reading about thieves? Writing about them? That's fun. And what's even more fun is writing about thieves living safely in the past who form an unlikely team and do good as they exercise their sticky-fingered vocation.

This book is set in 1913, which was a fascinating year in American history. World history, too. The year before the outbreak of the First World War people remained hopeful and optimistic while grappling with the rapid pace of political, social, and technological change. It was the acme of the progressive movement, which sought to reform American society and embraced such diverse causes as urban sanitation, childhood education, workplace safety, and ending political corruption.

The suffrage movement, the effort to win voting rights for women, entered its most dramatic phase. Having won voting rights in most western states, women set their sights on winning suffrage in populous eastern states, victories that would pave the way for a voting rights amendment to the Constitution. The era was also one of rapid technological change with airplanes, automobiles, and other technological marvels introduced over the previous decade.

Changes didn't reach everyone, and most folks still struggled. What better way to explore this era than through the eyes of thieves, but not just any thieves, but thieves who care.

Our crew of thieves, who call themselves the Barnacles, includes:

- Sapphire, a Mafia princess on the run from her ex-husband's gang.
- Jefferson, a shy, know-it-all safecracker.
- Lars, a cat burglar who can climb just about anything and wants to do it all the time.
- Missy, a suffragist who advocates stealing from the morally bankrupt to sell to the morally compromised.

- Oscar, an inventor/scientist doing crime as a way of making enough money for his experiments.
- And finally, the beautiful and mysterious captain of the crew, Captain Anne, who won't talk of her past or how she came to own the *Lighting Bug*, the best damn houseboat that ever floated down the Mississippi.

Join them for a rollicking ride down the river.

DEAD IN DUBUQUE

AUTHORS OF LIGHTNING SCARRED

C. S. STEIN

DEAD IN DUBUQUE

A BARNACLES SHORT STORY

Dead in Dubuque: *The idea for this story came while watching a television police procedural. Of course, that was serious. This is a bit more fun. It's told through Missy's point of view, the character that Steve finds most interesting and the most relatable. Missy is a thief with an iron-clad view of right and wrong. Stealing from evil people is the right thing to do in her estimation. But a job doesn't always go right, even when Missy is involved.*

DEAD IN DUBUQUE

Missy imagined she could smell death hanging in the air, like the dust liberally coating the red velvet curtains and falling through the beams of the high ceiling in the early morning light. Like death, the dust crept into the otherwise stately and well-kept home, unannounced and unwanted. It sparkled like tiny, golden damselflies and ticked Missy's nose.

She clenched her jaw and stifled a sneeze. She couldn't draw attention to herself. Or do anything out of character, anything to make the folks attending the funeral notice she wasn't just another servant. If all went well, the guests would think she'd been hired by the family. The family would think she was part of the funeral parlor staff. The funeral director shouldn't even notice her, focused as he was on the deceased and his relatives.

From what she could make out, the casket was upstairs. Captain Anne said he'd died two days ago. The family were rushing to get him into the ground. While summer in Dubuque wasn't as hot as it has been two years ago in 1911, it was still too hot and sticky to keep a corpse around for long.

Guests kept moving up and down the old home's stairs, which creaked under their weight. They were presumably going to, or coming from, paying their respects to the deceased. It was an unexpected wrench in the works.

Missy smoothed her borrowed uniform and lifted the silver tray of funeral sweets she'd found in the kitchen. The sugar cookies, embossed with a cherub's head, smelled delicious. A dutiful servant would never filch a taste, though. At least not in front of anyone. She'd already pulled enough cookies for her fellow Barnacles. She'd grab more before she left. Stealing was hard work, and one could never have enough cookies.

She silently offered the tray to a large dowager who grabbed three cookies without so much as a thank you and strode upstairs, chewing noisily. It occurred to her that everyone she'd seen was an adult. Was that normal for a funeral? She'd only been to the one, Great Aunt Ethel's, who died when she was still in school. Lots of children at that one.

Missy avoided meeting anyone's eyes, but listened intently, hoping for clues. She needed to find out where the safe was. Once the funeral began, they'd have 15 minutes to crack the safe, swap the real will with the forgery, grab anything worth grabbing, and get away.

That's when she felt the tap on her shoulder. "What are you doing down here?" It was a male voice, but not one that she recognized.

Her blood turned to ice. She made herself turn slowly, a smile on her face. A large man with full red cheeks in the garb of the local police loomed over her. "Sir?" she asked, trying to buy a bit of time. "Would you like a sweet?" She lifted her tray to him, changing the grip slightly, so she could fling it in his face if she needed to.

He took one of the cookies and smiled at her. "Think I can't recognize you in that get-up. I'd know you anywhere. What are you doing here? It's not safe."

She peered at him, flashing through a photo album of people in her mind. He didn't look at all familiar, but folks often confused her for someone else. Captain Anne told her she had that kind of face. "Of course! How could I forget you? You look so good I almost didn't recognize you. Have you been exercising?"

He smiled grimly. "You always were a sweet talker." He pulled out a pistol with one hand, waved it carelessly, and grabbed her elbow with the other. "Maybe another time, Toots. But for now, I'm going to do you a favor in honor of our relationship."

Relationship? What the hell was he up to? And who was he? Missy raked her gaze up his uniform and back down, noting the small discrepancies. The buttons didn't match one another. The shoes were brown, not black. He smelled of Kentucky whiskey. Any one of those things was a warning. All three together painted a picture of someone pretending to be a cop.

He holstered his pistol, pulled her close to him, and kissed her on the lips. His breath was sour and hot. Cheap whiskey. "That's a down payment until you meet me at Breitbach's tonight. Once me and my friends are finished here, you and me, we'll have some fun. But for now, you skedaddle, sweetheart. It's too hot for you here."

She allowed him to lead her out of the house, his hand still gripping her elbow. She batted her eyes and pretended to flirt with him as they walked. He pushed her out and closed the door behind her, winking as he did. She listened but didn't hear him lock the door behind her.

There was a bench on the porch, wood slats in a wrought iron frame, and she sank down onto it. Sweating in Dubuque's steamy morning heat, she took a bite of one of the cookies she'd pilfered for the team. As the sugar and flour melted in her mouth, realization dawned.

Mercy! Some other gang was trying to take their boodle. If they didn't move fast, the loot would be gone. Plus, if they couldn't get the will into the safe before tomorrow when the lawyer opened it, the will wouldn't be worth a hill of beans. The client wouldn't pay them. She'd hang up her fiddle before she'd let that happen.

She considered her options. Captain Anne was of no use. She was in the driver's seat of the getaway car, keeping it ready. The team wouldn't see her until it was time to leave. She was supposed to leave a note for Jefferson on the location of the safe and make a mark on the front of the gates to indicate she'd found it. She could leave a mark and then intercept him. But if she didn't have a location that wouldn't do much good, would it?

She leaned against bench, getting her face closer to the window, listening to the quiet hubbub of voices within and breathing in the sweet tannins of the maple trees that surrounded the house mingling with the dry rot of the planks of wood that made up the porch.

She had to find that safe. And fast.

Would it work to be someone else? She wished she'd stashed a second set of clothes, but she hadn't. She would just have to gut it out in her server costume. And she didn't have anyone to help her get into another outfit. She patted it down, feeling for the chalk, pen, and notepaper she'd stashed in the pinafore pocket. Still there.

She wrote a note to Jefferson, hoping the oblique 'Not yet' would make sense to him.

She pressed the note between the wood slats of the bench and considered her next move.

As she did, she heard a scream. Then another. And a gunshot. She prayed that no one had been harmed. She'd check on that and then take advantage of the chaos the gang had filled the scene with.

She felt the surge of excitement bubbling through her veins, focusing her mind, and drying her mouth. This could definitely work. Their newfound rivals would be their distraction. They could still get the job done, and no one would even realize they'd been there.

She grabbed the doorknob, but it didn't turn. The bastard had locked her out.

She slid over to the windows and peered in. A trio of cops, presumably fake, pointed guns amidst tumbled furniture and scattered people. They motioned the people toward the right, away from the front door. A woman dressed in opulent black lace ruffles, almost indecently lavish for a time of mourning, wailed loudly. The way she was dressed advertised that she was not one of those closest to the deceased. Missy thought she remembered her flirting with one of the men when she'd served cookies.

The man next to Lace Ruffles held a stovepipe top hat with a thick band indicating his closeness to the deceased. He must be a brother. His fashionable suit, gray trousers, black topcoat, and neatly buttoned suitcoat with a fancy watch chain, was rumpled and slightly torn at the shoulder. He clutched his left arm. His spectacles were awry. There must have been a tussle.

Missy's so-called relationship was in the middle of it all pointing his pistol at the man. She didn't see any blood, though. Maybe they hadn't shot anyone, just made a show of it. It made sense. Shooting someone was just as likely to cause a panic as to cow people and pretty much guaranteed the cops would get off their duffs and pursue them vigorously.

Holy smokes! How was she supposed to find the safe and how was Jefferson supposed to crack it with those chuckle-heads waving guns around? And what were they after?

She pulled out a duck caller from her pocket and made the "Mayday" call to alert Jefferson there was trouble. Then she sidled back to the front door, picked its lock, which opened to her fingers like a black-eyed Susan flower turning toward the sun. She slipped quietly inside.

The clamor of people talking in the drawing room was loud and angry, but no one seemed to be wailing from a serious injury. Still, she could smell the dank smell of fear.

She walked as quietly as she could in her boots, but they clicked on the hardwood floor whenever she moved away from the carpet runner. The stairs would certainly creak under her feet as they had under everyone else's.

One of the fake policemen spotted her and swung his pistol toward her. "Hey, who are you? What are you doing out here?"

She tried not to flinch. She was beginning to hate guns on this job. Or at least idiots with guns.

"I'm just the maid," she said. "I was supposed to serve cookies, but I snuck away for a break. Please don't tell on me, officer."

He looked around for a moment, clearly realized that she meant him a beat later, and then motioned her into the parlor. "You gotta stay with the rest of them. Get on in."

She was able to keep from rolling her eyes only with years of practice not calling out the idiocy of other people.

As near as she could tell the parlor was none the worse for wear since she'd been cooling her heels on the front porch. There were clearly signs of a struggle. The fancy red rug had wrinkled up in the corner and a lamp was still slantwise on the end table. People were huddled in groups of twos and threes talking in low voices and casting dark gazes at fake police and their fellow mourners.

Missy walked straight through as if she were the world's best maid and righted the lamp.

She looked around the room. No one would meet her eyes. Great! Instead of everyone thinking that she was part of the household or the funeral parlor, they thought she was a member of the gang. May as well make the best of it.

She turned to the woman with the lace ruffles. "You know, Ma'am, you should give them the information they want."

"Those ruffians?"

"Because they are ruffians." Missy cocked her head and lowered her voice. "If you know what I mean."

The woman turned red then pale then red again. "They keep asking for Joseph Wunder. But he's dead. We've all tried to explain that."

Missy blinked. "They want the corpse? Why?"

"I don't know. He's lying upstairs in ice. We told them that, too."

"Have you seen him?"

"I am of a delicate constitution. I cannot be exposed to death." She patted her eyes with a lace handkerchief.

Delicate as a rattlesnake, Missy thought but didn't say.

A hand pinched Missy's shoulder and roughly pulled her away. "I told you to skedaddle. What the hell's wrong with you? Can't you see we got serious business here?"

It was the fat fake police officer who thought she was some sort of dancehall girl or other past acquaintance of his. He was sweating and unlike the "delicate" woman with ruffles, he didn't smell like roses.

"I figured you could use some help. I can make you sandwiches or bring you cookies. Or whatever. Besides, you were taking so long and it's hot out there."

"Hot in here too," he said.

Missy nodded. "That lady says you're looking for a corpse."

"It's more complicated than that. A story for later. Go make those sandwiches. And bring cookies. Might as well get everyone fed." He motioned to one of his fellows to take her to the kitchen and told him to watch her.

It was clear that no one had been in the kitchen since Missy last pulled a tray of funeral cookies. The fresh smoked fish that was supposed to be served later was still sitting on its block of ice half filleted. The cook had probably been pulled into the parlor with everyone else. At least she hoped so. As near as she could tell the only person dead in this house was the guest of honor, the subject of the funeral. The strange crew didn't seem like cold-blooded killers. She wasn't sure what tipped her off to them, but she could feel a coldness in the hearts of those who made their living like maggots feeding on the dead bodies of others, and this crew didn't have that feel to them. Not that they were entirely good guys either. She'd reserve judgement. At least until tonight.

She looked around the kitchen, finding enough bread, cheese, fish, and meat to make adequate sandwiches. As she began slicing the bread, her guard cleared his throat. She looked up at him. He was grinning at her, looking about as young as he looked.

"So, you're sweet on Big Ed?" he asked, as if they were both in school jawboning on the playground.

Big Ed. That must be the big fake cop's name. "I ain't saying."

The man laughed. "I knew it. We all knew it."

"You can think as you like. Why not ask him?"

The man laughed again, clearly delighted with his "cleverness." This time Missy did roll her eyes. She turned back to the table, positioned just in front of the back door where she could keep an eye out.

She heard Jefferson's quiet footsteps on the back porch before she saw him. He nodded at her, his wiry frame moving silently as a ghost. At least as silently as a ghost could while wearing big clumpy work boots.

The man guarding her had started to look bored, like he wanted to get out of the kitchen. Missy smiled at him, doing her best to appear amiable and sweet, like someone who would have a relationship with Big Ed in the parlor. "Would you like some cookies? No reason for you to starve while waiting here."

He started to shake his head no, but she brought the tray close to him so that he could smell the fragrances of sugar and cinnamon. He looked down at the tray and in that moment, she shifted it so that he had to turn his head away from the back door.

Jefferson saw and slipped in unobserved. As he did, Missy dropped the tray, making it look like it was just too heavy for her.

"Oh dear! Oh, dear! Everyone will be so angry with me if the cookies break." She put her hands to her mouth and made her eyes go wide like Lillian Gish confronting horrors in the movie reels. "Oh goodness! Goodness me!"

From the outside a rough man's voice shouted, "What's going on in there?"

"She dropped the cookies," her guard shouted, turning to the door.

It was her chance. She grabbed a fist of cookies from her pinafore pocket and shoved them into his mouth.

As he struggled around her choking hand and crumbling cookies, Jefferson came from behind, pulled him down, just as quiet and quick as you please, and knocked him out. He whispered, "That's a Japanese technique I read about. Did you know that the human body has more than 300 pressure points? Some even talk about the Dim Mak, the touch of death."

Missy hushed him. No time for Jefferson's trivia now. "We need to get into the safe, switch the wills, and get out of here."

"Do you know where it is?"

"I think it must either be in the study or upstairs with the stiff."

The guard moaned. "Who are you?"

"So much for your pressure points. We better tie him up."

"Hey, wait," the guard mumbled. Missy grabbed a dishcloth and stuffed it in his mouth, while Jefferson shredded others and used the strips to secure the gag and bind the man's wrists and ankles. He struggled a little, but not too much. Maybe there was something to Jefferson's pressure points. Together, they dragged him to the pantry, shoved him in, and closed the door.

"We should split up and find the safe."

Missy nodded as she reassembled her tray. Some of the cookies were broken, but that couldn't be helped. Hopefully no one would notice. At least not in time to stop her. "I'll go first. I'll make a commotion. Once their attention is on me, you can get up the stairs. Then I'll check the study."

Jefferson nodded. "Where are the stairs?"

Missy motioned with her head. "The staircase is past the parlor. They've been going up and down it all day. It squeaks something fierce so be careful."

Jefferson did the weird finger stretching exercises he did sometimes. Missy rolled her eyes but didn't say anything. The man had an explanation for anything you could think of. Probably most of it was humbug. Even if it wasn't, she didn't want to get him started.

Jefferson looked like he was memorizing the house. In the seconds that felt like hours, Missy realized that they would have no way to contact each other if one of them found the safe. She waved her hands in negation. "I've changed my mind. We go together."

"I'm just trying to figure out the best route through. There's always a best way. It's math."

"Sure," she said quickly. "But I still think we should stick together. Easier to escape if we are together. Captain Anne always says stick together, doesn't she?"

"No. On our last job she had each of us in a different building. And there was also the Red Wing job. Remember that one?"

Missy didn't. She was the newest member of the crew, so she didn't doubt that things worked differently before she arrived and Jefferson, for all his smarts, didn't spend a lot of time focused on the crew. It had taken him weeks to even learn her name. "Well on this job, we stick together. Ready?"

"Which one? My calculations are that the study is more likely to hold a safe."

"But everyone's been going up and down those stairs all day," Missy said.

"Do you know what the gang wants here? Maybe we should take that first."

"They want the corpse."

"What? Why?"

Missy shrugged.

The study was on the way, and it had the benefit of having fewer people hanging around. Plus, Jefferson said he didn't want to work in front of the dead. It seemed disrespectful. Missy could see his point. So, they went there first.

The study looked like it had been designed by two people with radically different tastes. The center of the room was taken up with a massive old-fashioned carved desk with birds as supports. It had a pile of papers, as if someone had shuffled through them. One wall was entirely taken up with a bookcase so covered with antique statuary that there was barely room for books. The rest of the furniture was modern, so were the paintings on the wall. Beautiful Art Deco works. Behind the desk was their quarry: the safe.

Jefferson knelt before it, repeating his weird little hand exercises.

"Hurry!"

"I need to concentrate. Watch for intruders."

It took him five excruciating minutes to open the safe. Missy used the time to pocket some of the more enticing bits of bric-a-brack and suck on one of the cookie pieces still left in her pinafore pocket. Hopefully something would make this trip worthwhile.

The snick of the safe opening was such a relief, Missy let go of a sigh. "Is it there?"

"Sure is. And there's —"

At that moment a great hubbub erupted from the parlor, followed by screams and shouting. And a gunshot.

She grabbed Jefferson's hand. "Make the switch and let's go."

"You think someone is hurt?"

"I think we are the ones who will be hurt if we're still here in a few minutes. Go! Remember, switch the wills but leave everything in the safe. It has to look untouched."

Jefferson made the switch.

They ran out of the study together and straight into two older women. Before she could slip aside, one of them grabbed Missy's arm and tugged her toward the stairs.

"At last! The maid. Where have you been? Never mind. I don't care. My dead husband has come back to life. You need to clean his room."

"That's right," the other woman confirmed, her lips set in a firm line.

Missy struggled for a moment and then, realizing what the women had said, stopped. "What?"

"You heard me! Get upstairs and clean his room." She pushed Missy toward the stairs.

Missy grabbed the banister to keep from tripping on the staircase and headed upstairs to get away from the wild-eyed women. None of this made any sense, but maybe there would be something worth pocketing up there.

Jefferson stretched his fingers and followed her upstairs. They picked up their pace as the sounds of further commotion reached them from the bedroom.

When they entered the bedroom, the strong smell of hothouse lilies hit her. They were piled on every surface and around the plain wood coffin that occupied the room's center. The coffin's lid was overturned and on the floor. Beside it was a shattered flower vase and more lilies, which must have filled the vase and covered the coffin before someone flipped over its lid. Someone strong. It was thick, heavy wood.

Around the room people shouted and pointed at one another.

The coffin itself was empty, not even any ice, which was what everyone was shouting about.

"It's a miracle."

"No, it's some kind of con."

"No, he probably was just mostly dead. I've heard about folks that were accidentally buried alive. That's why they used to bury folks with bells so they could ring for help if they woke up in the grave."

"There ain't no way that Joseph Wunder deserves a miracle. If the good Lord wanted to gift a miracle, he'd be better off gifting it to the dogs than to that son of a bitch."

"Hush! Don't speak ill of the dead."

"He's not dead."

Jefferson slid amongst the people looking like he belonged. "That's right," he said. Who he was agreeing with Missy didn't know but she bent to pick up the scattered lilies. Might as well act like a maid as she assessed the situation.

The room bubbled with people moving in and out and crowding against each other. Distracted as they were, it might be possible to relieve some of them of their jewelry. But dressed as a maid? No. Too risky. She was bound to be yelled at, or worse, if she brushed against someone.

Missy glanced around. A vase of more lilies and a short-barreled revolver occupied a small table near the casket. A leather-covered valet tray rested atop a bureau that might be worth searching. Those often held small valuables like watches and cufflinks. The bed had been pushed against the far wall and wasn't worth searching. On the other side of the room she saw a small vanity was covered with various perfume bottles and atomizers as well as eye shadow palettes and tubes of lipstick and compacts. In its center sat a cardboard box containing Eglantine's Best Lavender-Scented Powder. Two drawers promised more valuable items inside, perhaps jewelry, if the owner wasn't wearing it all. Unfortunately, one of the guests sat in the vanity's chair, which they'd turned to face into the room.

Missy gathered more the lilies and arranged them in the vase near the revolver. As she did, she took in the crowd of people. They looked straight through her as if she were part of the furniture and continued to argue with one another. No one notices a maid. Unless, of course, they had a dirty job that needed doing.

None of the people she saw looked like a reanimated corpse. Thank the Lord! Where had the formerly dead subject of the funeral gone?

As Missy watched Jefferson sidled up to a small group. He was much better at picking locks than dipping into people's pockets, but he looked like he was going to try. As he turned to use his body to shield his questing fingers, though, another guest came from behind him. Missy shook her head, trying to warn Jefferson, but he was focused on his target.

Missy shrieked. "Oh Lord! Is that the dead man?" she asked, pointing away from Jefferson toward a skinny guy talking up one of the women. Seriously, who looks for a date at a funeral?

Everyone turned to look, and Jefferson completed his snatch. He definitely needed more practice.

"No, you dizzy dodo," a tall man said "He isn't in here anymore. See the empty coffin?"

Missy made a show of looking at the coffin and then back to the skinny guy as if she were slow and trying to make the calculations.

"It's so hard to find good help these days," a woman commented.

Sympathetic murmurs of agreement spread through the room, as numerous well-dressed guests favored Missy with looks of varying degrees of disapproval.

Missy hung her head as if she were embarrassed.

Meanwhile, Jefferson sidled up to the table, picked up the revolver and toyed with it.

Missy again shook her head at him, warning him off. What was he thinking grabbing a gun?

Jefferson gave her quick smile, replaced the gun on the table, and sauntered into the crowd, hands in his pockets.

Good. Hopefully, he'd stick to safecracking and leave pickpocketing to her, at least until he got better at it. Maybe she'd show him a few things once they were back aboard the Lightning Bug, their houseboat home.

The loud report of a gun interrupted Missy's musings on what to teach Jefferson. It came from downstairs. What was going on?

The milling crowd backed away from the room's doorway just as Big Ed ran through it and ducked into the crowd.

Close behind Big Ed came another man, taller and thinner than Big Ed and wearing an expensive, but too tight suit. He yelled and waved a baseball bat and shouted "Where is he? I'm going to get him!"

"You're supposed to be dead," Big Ed yelled back. "What the hell's going on?" He ducked behind the empty coffin just in front of Missy.

"It's father!" a woman in a somber, black dress said. "He really is alive. How is that possible?" she gasped and then swooned into the arms of her conveniently nearby male companion.

"Joseph?" asked another man. "How are you alive?"

Joseph Wunder, the very lively corpse, waved his bat toward the casket and shouted "Yes, I'm alive. Now shut up and tell me the money is or you're going to need this casket."

Big Ed seized that moment to make his move. He dodged behind Missy, reached the side table in a few quick strides and grabbed the gun. Pointing it at Joseph, he demanded "Put down the bat. You're the one who owes us money, and we ain't leaving without it. You don't want to wind up dead for real, do you?"

A women screamed in what seemed to Missy an excessively theatrical fashion, but at least it got everyone's attention. She needed to calm things down. Missy stepped between the two men and turned toward Big Ed. "I know you're a lover not a fighter."

"I can be both. Now get out of the way."

Missy turned fully toward him, crossed her arms, and glared. "You're not going to kill anyone today. Not in front of me."

"I told you this was too hot for a baby doll like you. Now just stop with the banana oil and let me take care of this. This guy owes me money—a lot of money."

Jefferson moved to Missy's side between the two men. "You're going to have to shoot both of us," he said boldly.

Missy gave him a disgusted look. This wasn't the way to handle it.

Big Ed gestured toward several of his fellow fake cops who'd entered the room. "Get those two out of here."

Three of them rushed forward. Two grabbed Jefferson, one on either side, and hustled him toward the door. The third, the one they'd left tied in the kitchen, grabbed Missy's right arm and dragged her along.

"Vengeance is mine," he hissed.

"Isn't that supposed to be reserved for the Lord?"

"Not anymore."

"Now," Big Ed said, "We settle this."

"Let's go, Missy," Jefferson said, as he shook off the bruisers and exited the room. "We don't want to be here for what happens next." He grabbed Missy's other arm and pulled her from her escort who was already turning back toward the room to watch the showdown.

"But..."

He rattled something that sounded suspiciously like bullets in his pocket. "We got what we came here for."

Halfway down the stairs they heard a masculine whine, "What? Empty? No bullets?" Someone shouted. Others shouted back. Something crashed, perhaps another vase, and Missy heard the distinctive wet smack of someone's fist hitting a face. Jefferson pulled her down the last few steps as the room above erupted into a cacophony of violence.

Days later Missy and her fellow Barnacles finally found out what happened. Jefferson had picked up a newspaper at their last stop. He called them together the *Lightning Bug's* upper deck and summarized the story as their faithful houseboat drifted down the Mississippi. A gentle breeze cooled their skin.

"So, there wasn't a corpse?"

"The stiff was very much alive. Apparently, it was a trap to draw in his competition."

"Seems to have worked. That gang was fooled."

"Everyone was fooled," Jefferson said.

Captain Anne nodded. "Glad you guys got out of there. Too bad that switching the will is pointless since the guy was still alive."

Missy frowned. "That's really not fair. We did the job."

"Sure."

"And we should get paid," Missy said. "I'm still new at this, but that's how it works, right? You do the job and then you get paid."

"In a perfect world," Anne said, taking a sip of lemonade. "Though in a perfect world folks wouldn't need us to swap out forged wills nor would there be a place for thieves like us, would there?"

"The client owes us another job then."

Captain Anne nodded.

A few months later Missy learned just what that job would be. But that's a story for another day.

CRACKING CAIRO

AUTHORS OF LIGHTNING SCARRED
C. S. STEIN
CRACKING
CAIRO
A BARNACLES SHORT STORY

Cracking Cairo: *Steve is a naval historian with a keen interest in the ancient world. When we came across a discussion of Greek pottery in connection with the ancient vessels we tucked it away for future stories. This story connects that ancient pot to the Civil War and then to 1913. But is that the real treasure? This story features Jefferson, the team's introverted safe cracker, and Lars, a cat burglar and thrill seeker.*

CRACKING CAIRO

The river stank.

Which is not to say the Ohio River ever smelled particularly wholesome, not like the rivers near Lars' home in Minnesota.

Factories, warehouses, mines, granaries, and slaughter-houses lined the Ohio River. It was an industrial river and smelled like one. Upstream, coal smoke mixed with manure and rotting animal flesh and assorted agricultural and industrial residues to create a cloying miasma.

But here, just north of Cairo at the southern tip of Illinois where the Ohio emptied into the Mississippi River, the stench was of a different order. Maybe it was the season or maybe it was something about the currents in this stretch of water, but the most foul-smelling green sludge grew here. It piled up on the banks where Captain Anne had anchored their houseboat, the *Lightning Bug*. It was both their home and their getaway vehicle. As much as Lars was coming to loath Cairo, he loved their little boat.

Lars pinched his nose, trying to avoid breathing in as much as possible as he walked along the muddy shore. It almost made him regret leaving his family's farm. "Anne, why here? This place stinks to high heaven."

That had been a mistake. The second he drew a breath in to speak he tasted the overpowering reek of dead fish and wet, moldy, rotting vegetation. He gulped, hoping the score was worth this.

Captain Anne Harris didn't look at him. She just continued to stare into the dense growth along the river. Her voice, when she finally responded, was soft, yet firm, like Miss Spencer, a schoolteacher Lars remembered from his childhood. "Yeah, and people around here aren't that nice either. Cairo's had hard times since the railroads passed it by last century, and hard times make folks mean. There were lynchings a couple years ago, 1910, I think. Ida Wells investigated but couldn't get anyone to pay attention. Anyone with any sense is leaving for greener pastures."

Lars nodded.

"But," she continued, "we're not here to make friends or enjoy the scenery. We're here to do a job. The town's decaying and the cops are overworked and underfunded. That works for us."

Anne pulled a glossy sheet of paper from her pocket and unfolded it. A page torn from a magazine, it showed a painting of several glittering antebellum mansions, their grand porticos and peaked roofs shaded by cypress and tupelo trees and a few magnolias. "This is Millionaires Row, a couple miles down the river from us. Mansions built back when Cairo was flush. It will smell a lot better there."

"You think?"

"Even if it doesn't," she continued smoothly, "the smell of money freshens the air wonderfully, don't you think? Those families made a killing trading cotton before the Civil War and profiteering during it. Now they exploit local farmers and sharecroppers. Our target's the one on the right." She tapped the page. "The Red Camellia. They say President Grant stayed there back in the day. The client wants us to grab an antique vase they have. Anything else we find is ours for the taking."

"Won't people be there? If not the family, the servants?"

Anne shrugged. "Client claims the house will be empty. No family. No servants. I guess we'll find out."

Lars stared at the page and then up at the vines covering the nearby trees, so dense and tangled it was impossible to determine the species of either or to figure out a way through them to the town. It was as if a vast, monstrous mass of vegetation was dying but desperately wanted to strangle every living thing to death before it passed on. He shuddered. Rather than industry, Mother Nature herself, it seemed, had cursed this place. He wished they'd never come.

Anne was right, though. Do the job and then get out of town. Coast down the last stretch of the Ohio River to the Mississippi, avoiding local cops, state troopers, and anyone else harboring petty grievances against them.

"Ahem," a voice said behind them. "That your boat?"

Lars spun around along with Anne who slipped the magazine page behind her back.

A balding, middle-aged man with dark, weatherbeaten skin stood in the dense shadows of the trees. He pointed at their boat with his walking stick. "Yours?" he repeated, continuing to point.

Before they could answer, he continued. "You can't anchor here. Private property. Not mine you understand. Just passing through myself, but folks are touchy 'round here. Anything could set 'em off, especially a bunch of strangers in a houseboat hiding in the woods. Folks will think you're up to no good."

"Not us," Anne smiled. "We just needed to stop and stretch our legs for a spell."

"We'll be back on the river in just a couple of shakes of something or other," Lars added, trying to sound cheerful.

The man looked dubious but smiled. "Well, that's alright then. Best to be back on your boat before nightfall." He gave a half-hearted wave and turned to go.

"Wait," Anne said. She reached into a pocket and handed him a few coins. "You look like you could use them."

"Can't we all? That's awful kind of you." He pocketed the coins and retreated smoothly back into the woods, avoiding the entangling vines.

"Do you think he believed us?" asked Lars.

"Would you?"

"So, back on the boat?"

"Back aboard. Let Missy and Jefferson know we're moving up the timetable. And then we're getting the hell out of here. A handful of coins may keep that gentleman from talking, but we shouldn't count on it."

The mansion loomed against the night sky as the team gathered under a tall cypress tree. The full moon illuminated the mansion's garden despite Cairo's nighttime haze. Unfortunately, the moon would also illuminate them as they crossed the grounds and sought entry, checking doors and windows.

Lars strode over to the wrought iron fence surrounding the house and paced along it, peering through its cemetery-like bars. Best not to think about that. Bad luck to think of death on a job.

Anne thought the family were up the street at some coming out party. Lars hoped so. Something felt wrong though. He sniffed the air. It was fresh here, smelling of magnolias and camellias, but also moldering soil and something else, something wild. He returned to Anne under the tree, padding gently on the soft, wet earth. "Are there dogs?"

"Client didn't say."

"I think we would know if the place had guard dogs," Jefferson put in. "Most folks would leave them out front when they were gone. We'd probably hear them."

Missy shuddered.

"Hmmm," Anne said. "Best to be safe. We have time. Take a few minutes and walk the perimeter, Missy. Attract the attention of any dogs, but carefully. Don't get caught."

Missy nodded and tied a scarf over her hair. She looked grim, like a warrior entering battle. Lars didn't blame her. Four years ago, Cairo had lynched a black man and ghoulishly handed out pieces of his heart. Missy didn't like working jobs in the South, and while Cairo wasn't technically in the Old South, it was damned close, particularly in folks' attitudes.

"Lars, you work along the fence in the other direction. Do you have the crowbar and tools?"

"All in my satchel."

"Good, we should avoid the front gate. With everyone coming and going from the party there's too much chance of being seen from the street. Look for a place we can pry apart a few bars and squeeze through. And here," she added, passing him the magazine page she'd shown him earlier. "Take this. If you can spot the vase through a window, things will go quicker once we're inside."

Lars set off, studying the fence in the moonlight as he walked. He turned the corner and continued along the fence on the home's southern side. After a few dozen yards, near the back of the house, he found a good spot. Water seeped along the supporting brickwork and weakened the mortar. It would be easy to pry out two or three bars here, creating a gap through which people and loot could move. One of the bars even looked like it was rusting at the bottom, though it was hard to tell in the moonlight.

Mission accomplished, Lars stepped back and studied the magazine page. Not the front, which showed the mansions, but the back, which had pictures of their interiors and a close-up of their prize, a pottery vase. An amphora, Jefferson called it. Red on black or black on red, Lars couldn't remember. What mattered is that it was old and Greek and valuable. Rich folks loved old Greek stuff.

Judging by the picture, it sat on a fireplace mantle in plain sight. The Harrison family grabbed it during the Civil War— stole it from some slave plantation across the border whose owners took off just ahead of the Union Army.

That got Missy's attention at the briefing. "So, the morally compromised stole it from the morally bankrupt, and now we're stealing it from them?"

Everyone laughed.

Their client was probably morally compromised, too, that being the nature of clients, but nothing as unseemly as what seemed the norm around Cairo. They'd bag the vase for the client and help themselves to anything else interesting in the house.

Lars pulled the crowbar from his satchel and got to work on the bars, the first of which snapped cleanly at its base. Rusted all the way through. He set his crowbar against the next bar and leaned. It groaned.

Suddenly, Lars heard the high-pitched sound of yapping dogs, an aborted scream that sounded like Missy, and more high-pitched barking and yapping. Not just one dog but several. It came from the other side of the mansion.

He dashed around the corner, rounded the back of the house, and ran toward Missy's shout. The ground was wet and uneven, and his feet squelched through patches of dank, slimy mud. Ahead, shadows moved and writhed and barked, tearing at something on the ground.

Missy!

Lars loped toward her, hopped over a large patch of mud that glittered in the moonlight, and picked up his pace as the ground firmed. He was almost to Missy when something grabbed his ankle.

He tripped, twisted as he fell, rolled twice, and ended up on his back. The satchel of tools fell beside him with a wet splat that sprayed mud and muck into his eyes. He could hear Missy a few feet from him, giggling.

Giggling?

Something wet nudged Lars's face, and he screamed.

"Quiet," Missy said in a loud whisper.

"But there's dogs. We gotta get out of here." Lars made to get up, but something landed on his chest.

"They're not dogs, they're puppies, and they're friendly."

Lars looked down his chest. A black and brown puppy with big floppy ears looked back at him, considered for a moment, and licked his face. Apparently happy with what it found, it began licking industriously, until Lars gently pushed it back down his chest and began petting it.

Missy fed something to one of the puppies crawling on her. It chewed noisily, swallowed, and nudged her hand, eager for more. "We should take them with us," Missy said, trying to pet all the puppies at once. There must be a half dozen of them.

"We're thieves, not dognappers. We can't just run off with someone's puppies. What if they belong to some kid?"

Just then, something growled. Something definitely not a puppy.

A large German shepherd glared at them and bared its teeth, a fearsome noise coming through from the other side of the wrought iron fence. It tried to squeeze its head between the bars but managed only its snout, which it soon withdrew. It continued to growl and glare, focusing more attention on Lars than Missy, which seemed unfair. He'd just gotten there.

"I think it's their mother," Missy said.

"You think?"

"I'll give her a treat. Maybe she's friendly, too."

"Are you nuts? She'll bite your hand off. And where did you get all this food for the dogs?"

Missy, though, was already in motion. "Anne gave me a bunch of meat scraps from dinner. That's why she sent me ahead." She offered the enormous dog a one of the scraps, holding it carefully, just outside the bars.

The dog growled, advanced, and stuck her nose through the bars to sniff the treat. Then, it whined and retreated. That was strange.

Missy continued to encourage the dog, cooing and showing the dog the treat. She licked her lips and made yummy sounds. "Don't you want it?" she asked. "It's very good."

Rather than growling, the dog now looked puzzled. It advanced, whined piteously, and retreated.

"Well," Lars said, "she's not a guard dog. She's afraid of us. And," Lars added, taking a closer look, "she's awfully skinny for a guard dog, or any dog, really."

"Yeah, Missy replied, peering through the bars, "I think you're right. And the puppies are starving. I can't give them food fast enough. I'm running out. Maybe they're strays."

"How'd she get inside the fence then?"

"Hopped over it looking for food? I don't know." Missy peered closer. "She's awfully big. I bet she could hop this fence, but she's favoring one paw. Maybe she hurt herself jumping over."

"What do we tell Anne? We have no idea how the dog will react when we go through the fence."

The subject of the conversation looked quizzically at Lars for a moment and then turned back to Missy's proffered treat. The dog advanced a step, and another, and paused. Suddenly, the dog lunged forward, grabbed the treat from Missy's hand, and backed away, growling and chewing.

Two of the puppies, attracted by the sounds, scampered from Missy through the fence to their mother. After trying to filch a piece of her treat, they gamboled around her happily.

"We are definitely taking these puppies," Missy said. "And their mother, too." She pulled another treat from her pocket, held it out, but then thought better. "I only have two pieces of meat left. We need to get them to follow us."

"What makes you think they'll follow us?"

"The puppies will follow me. We're friends. And mom will follow her puppies," she said, as if it were obvious and she did this every day, the Pied Piper of Puppies.

Missy turned toward the large dog. "Won't you mom? Don't you want to come with us? We'll take care of you and your puppies and get you a warm place to sleep and feed you lots and lots of treats." She waved one of her remaining meat scraps to emphasize the point.

The dog looked dubious. Interested, perhaps, but definitely dubious.

Missy clapped her hands and called to the puppies, who happily ran over to her. Now their mother looked really dubious. "Come on Lars," she said, "grab your tools. We need to widen the fence for their mom."

"Are you sure about this? She's an awful big dog, even underfed as she is. What's to stop her from deciding that we're more appetizing than the scraps you're offering? In fact, what happens when you run out of food for them? You said you only had two pieces left."

"Two is more than enough for now. We'll probably find food for them in the mansion. If not, I'll feed them when we get to the boat. Now," she said, changing her tone, "get to it. We're already late getting back to Anne, and we need to rescue these puppies. It's the right thing to do."

When did she get so bossy? Lars grabbed his begrimed satchel, shook some of the mud off, and pulled out the crowbar. The fence looked in much better shape on this side of the house. This was not going to be easy.

Lars stuck the crowbar between two bars and leaned on it. They didn't move. He adjusted his grip, braced himself against the nearby brick pillar and pushed again. This time the bars had the decency to groan, but they barely moved. Maybe half an inch.

"Unless you have a longer crowbar, it's going to take both of us. Let the puppies fend for themselves a minute and give me a hand."

Anne saw them first. "What the hell?"

"We took care of the dogs," Missy grinned.

"Why are they following you?"

"They're strays," Lars said, trying to be helpful.

It was Jefferson who asked the obvious question. "How are we supposed to sneak into the mansion with a half dozen yapping puppies following us?"

"I'll stay here with the puppies and keep watch," Missy said. "You don't need me to find the vase."

"Amphora," Jefferson grumbled.

Anne looked a bit annoyed that Missy was giving orders but accepted the decision. "Alright, let's go."

Missy called after them. "Be sure to bring back some food for the puppies and their mom. Rich family with ancient amphoras is bound to have something good in the kitchen."

"This way," Lars said before Jefferson could debate the wisdom of looking for dog food in the middle of a robbery. "We won't fit through the gap we made for the dogs. There's a better spot on the other side of the house." He pointed in the opposite direction from which he and Missy had returned with the dogs. "Follow me."

As expected, the mansion was richly furnished, particularly the living room where Anne, Jefferson, and Lars gathered after entering through an unlocked window. There were life-sized statues in the corners and gold-framed paintings on the walls. Heavy, well-upholstered furniture dominated the room's center, clustered around a beautiful cloisonne coffee table, probably imported from China. Sconces for gas lights lined the walls, but the family had recently installed an enormous electric chandelier that looked like it needed a hundred bulbs.

Turning that on, Lars thought, would be like sending up a signal flare.

They clustered around the enormous fireplace and Jefferson played his light across its mantle. Its bare mantle.

They stared.

"Where's the amphora?" Jefferson asked.

"Spread out and find it," said Anne. "Place this big and this old will have fireplaces in most rooms."

Jefferson sprinted up the wide, curving staircase, ignoring the banister, and taking the steps two at a time. Anne went to the right and Lars to the left.

He checked the dining room and then the parlor next door. There was a nice upright piano in the parlor and a large mahogany table, a dozen chairs, and a sideboard in the dining room. The latter contained some very nice dishes, which they couldn't take, and silverware for at least a dozen place settings, which they could. Both rooms had fireplaces with mantles. Neither had the amphora, just family portraits and glittering knickknacks.

Lars helped himself to a few of the latter. Pocket anything small and shiny. Figure out its value later.

The kitchen was nearby. Probably no fireplace there, but Missy had asked about food for her new, hopefully temporary, pets. Besides, some folks hid stuff in the icebox. Best to check. Lars's stomach rumbled at the smell of the half-loaf of bread on the table.

There were actually three iceboxes. Two small, older ones, and a brand new electric one. Lars had heard about them, but never seen one. It hummed when he opened it and began rifling through a selection of cheeses and other farm produce.

It turned out the Harrisons didn't hide things in their iceboxes, but they were well stocked with ham, bacon, and other meats for Missy's dogs. Lars was setting out a selection of them on the counter to thaw when he heard Anne exclaim "Damn!" and then her whispered call "Found it."

Lars rushed back, meeting Jefferson on the way. Anne called again, and they found her back in the living room.

"We already checked this room," Jefferson said. "No amphora."

Anne pointed toward a shadowed corner. "Shine your light over there. What do you see?"

What they saw in the light was not the statue they expected, but an enormous clay pot on which two life-sized figures, outlined in red, did battle with shield and spear. The pot rested on a carved wooden platform that resembled the home's fireplace mantels.

"Well," Jefferson said, "the Greeks made amphora in many different sizes. They mostly stored wine and olive oil in them. They used some of the big ones for headstones on graves."

Anne sighed.

Lars felt her pain. He'd been paired with Jefferson for more jobs than seemed fair, and the man couldn't stop talking. If he wasn't asking questions, he was recounting "little known facts" no one actually wanted to know. The less important something was, the more important it was for Jefferson to know about it. If he could make money knowing trivia, Jefferson wouldn't need to steal.

"That's going to be the headstone on our grave," replied Lars. "How are we going to get it out of here? It's gotta be six feet tall."

"Wrap it in a rug and roll it?"

"Are you crazy?" said Anne. "It's a priceless antiquity."

"A priceless antiquity that ain't going nowhere" said Lars. "It's not like we brought a car or a horse cart."

"Hard to fit those on a houseboat," said Jefferson. "We need something else."

"Hey, I like the *Lightning Bug*," Lars said. "She's home."

"Yeah," Anne agreed. "The cops haven't gotten close to us once, since we picked up the *Bug*, made her our home, and took to the rivers." She looked up at the amphora. "Living on a boat, though, does present a problem when the client doesn't tell you the ancient pot you're stealing is taller than you are."

"And wider," added Jefferson.

"Yeah, I don't think it'll fit down the passageway below deck. We'll have to wrap it in blankets, cover it, and lash it on deck. Probably safest near the stern."

"First we have to get it to the boat," Jefferson said. "We'll have to widen the gap in the fence. How much do you think it weighs?

"It's a clay pot," said Lars. "It's hollow. Even that big, you and I can carry it."

"It would weigh more with olive oil in it, but you're right. It's not capped, so it's probably empty. Regardless, we can't carry it half a mile down the street to the boat."

"You got a better idea? We're running out of time. The family will be back soon."

"Hey," Anne said. "We're not carrying it down the street. Someone's bound to see us. More importantly, we can't take the risk of one of you losing his grip and dropping it. We can't so much as chip this ancient pot."

"So," asked Lars, "what's the plan?"

"I think I have an idea," Anne said. "Let's check out back behind the house. Old mansion like this is bound to have stables or a shed or two out back. Let's see what we find. Maybe they left us a horse and buggy."

"Yeah," Lars said, "I saw a shed when I was running over to Missy. Should I bring my tools?"

"Yep, let's go take a look."

The door squeaked softly as Anne carefully pushed it open and entered the shed. It was large and well-kept, not at all what Lars expected.

Pale shafts of moonlight filtered through the siding and roof beams. It was surprisingly clean for an outdoor shed with no dust on the surfaces or in the air. In fact, it was cleaner than the home's kitchen. Though instead of food and grease, it smelled of motor oil, ground steel, and freshly cut wood, without Cairo's ever-present smell of greenery and mildew.

A work bench along one wall held neatly arranged tools in several wooden boxes behind which sat a dozen mason jars filled with nails and screws of various sizes. Whoever used this shed, took their work seriously. Lars was impressed. The tools were good quality and would fetch a nice price from any pawn dealer.

In the shed's center, a tan oilcloth tarp covered something large.

Lars whistled. "The place practically sparkles. I wonder if they have a maid for their shed."

"Someone cares more about the things in here than they do about the treasures in the house. Let's see what they're hiding." Anne folded up one end of the tarp, revealing the front of a cherry red vehicle, but one unlike any Lars had seen before.

"That's a pretty strange looking automobile. It is an automobile, right?" he asked dubiously.

Anne smiled with satisfaction and a smidgeon of greed. "Well, well, well! Someone is a tinkerer. Or knows a tinkerer," she said as she pulled the tarp away further to reveal more of the strange vehicle. She ran her hand across its hood, bent close to it, and crooned, "Momma loves you."

"What is it?" asked Lars.

Anne lifted the hood and ran her hand along the engine. "Home-built roadster. Nice lines and a powerful engine — more horsepower than any car needs. Some strange accessories, though."

"What are those?" Lars pointed to what looked like short, wooden wings.

Anne fingered one and pushed. It folded neatly on itself and slid into a compartment under the car's chassis. "Don't quite know. Can't imagine why anyone would put wings on a car. They'd have to be enormous to get a car off the ground, not short like these. No time to puzzle through it now. We'll figure it out on the road."

"On the road? Have you ever driven one of these before?"

An excited girlish laugh escaped Anne, which was just a bit disconcerting coming from his normally staid Captain. "Of course not! No one has. It doesn't even look finished. It has four wheels, an engine, and a steering wheel, though. As long as it starts, we'll be fine. This sweetie is just what we need to transport the amphora and the rest of our loot. And Missy's puppies, since she seems determined to keep them."

Lars groaned.

"Pull this tarp off the rest of the way. Then, I'll need you to help crank this baby up."

Lars whipped off the tarp in a smooth motion, tossed it in a corner, and opened the driver's side door. Bending, he felt along the car's interior. "I can't find the crank. Shouldn't they keep it in the car?"

Anne opened a small door in front of the wing and felt around. "This should be the crankcase, but there's no slot for a crank, just a bunch of strange looking batteries." She leaned into the car next to Lars and probed inside, feeling along the car's interior.

"What are you doing?"

"Have you ever heard of a push button starter?"

Lars shook his head.

"I read about it in the paper. The new Cadillacs have them. It's like those new electric cash registers you've seen." She looked thoughtful for a moment. "Huh! That's what the batteries are for."

"We're not really going to drive this, are we?"

"Can you think of a better way to get our prize to the *Lighting Bug*?"

Lars couldn't, though he had a bad feeling about this. He'd read about automobiles turning turtle and killing everyone inside. More commonly, they broke down at the worst possible times, like when you're driving out of town with a bunch of stolen loot.

"It's the best way. Go tell Jefferson and have him help you carry out the pot. I'll get this baby started and meet you at the back door. We'll load the pot and then grab what loot we can in a few minutes."

Captain Anne looked entirely too happy about this situation. Normally Lars was all for happiness and fun, but this situation seemed like it could turn deadly in a New York minute.

"OK," Lars pointed. "Grab the tools before you head out. They're a damn sight better than what we have on the *Lightning Bug*."

"Agreed," Anne said as the car's engine rumbled to life. She grinned at Lars and waved him on. "Get going. Tick tock and all that."

Lars tossed his satchel into their newly acquired car and dashed back to the mansion to look for Jefferson and anything else he'd missed in his first run-through of the house.

The jewelry box was displayed prominently on the bureau in the large bedroom upstairs. He noted the safe in the bedroom, hidden in a large armoire. He considered telling Jefferson, but then heard the roar of the motorcar as Anne pulled up at the back door. What a godawful noise! They'd be lucky if they escaped with no one hearing them.

He ran down the stairs, his pockets jingling with a watch chain and several jewelry chains and rings. "Jefferson! We need to get the pot out to Captain Anne."

Jefferson appeared in the hallway, holding what looked like a sausage sandwich. He had a ham and two links of sausage dangling from his left arm and a rasher of bacon wrapped in butcher paper in his right. He'd never tagged Jefferson for a thief. At least not a thief of his friends' hard-stolen meat.

"Seriously? You're stealing my meat? I'm the one who set it out." He took the bacon from Jefferson and stuck it in his own pocket.

"For the puppies. And for dinner," he added at Lars' dubious look. "Did you find a safe? I couldn't find one down here."

"No time! We have to get the pot to Anne."

"Amphora," Jefferson corrected, yet again. Thankfully, he was too distracted to add whatever additional trivia he had squirreled away.

"You think it will work to wrap it in one of the quilts from upstairs?"

"It's better than nothing," Jefferson said.

Lars ran back upstairs and grabbed three quilts from a cedar chest smelling strongly of rose potpourri and mothballs. Lars suppressed a momentary need to sneeze.

Together Lars and Jefferson wrapped two of the quilts around the pot to cushion it and then rolled it onto the third, which they used as an improvised stretcher to carefully lift it and carry it toward the back door. Getting it out the narrow back door proved impossible. Instead, they opened the largest kitchen window and passed it through that to Captain Anne who left the car to help.

This turned out to be a problem. Almost as soon as Anne left the car, it choked twice and died.

"What is that?" Jefferson asked. "It doesn't look like any automobile I've ever seen."

Anne smiled up at Jefferson. Lars thought she was secretly enjoying knowing more about something than their resident know-it-all, but if she was, she didn't say it. "Isn't it fun? We think it's some inventor's project. Place the amphora in the backseat and I'll start her up again."

They squeezed the amphora slantwise into the backseat, leaving just enough room for Missy and the puppies, if the puppies and their mother cooperated. Lars and Jefferson would have to squeeze together into the front passenger seat. Fortunately, it was a short drive to the *Lightning Bug*.

Anne pressed the starter again, but nothing happened. She removed the front seat cushion and checked the level of some fluid. Lars couldn't tell what it was. Then she flicked a switch under the seat before pressing a button under the dashboard.

Still nothing.

Anne cursed and got out of the car.

Lars and Jefferson exchanged worried looks.

"What's wrong with you two. Out! We need to push it."

Jefferson shook his head as he stepped out of the back seat, steadying the amphora as he did. "What's the point of pushing it? Doesn't that defeat the whole purpose of automobiles. They're supposed to carry us. Not vice versa."

"Lars, you're stronger than Jefferson. You get on the other side. Jefferson, you're in the back of the car. When I say push, you push. Got it?"

Lars took his position holding onto the car's metal frame. In this position he could smell the seat leather and the slight smell of gasoline.

Jefferson grumbled, "I still don't get it," but he put his shoulder to the frame and pushed when Captain Anne said to.

"We need to get it up that slope and then push it down so that we can start it."

Jefferson took a breath and at first Lars thought they were in for more argument, but apparently, he thought better of it. He just grunted and pushed it up the slope.

Once at the top, Anne said, "OK. We need just one more push to get this thing moving. From there it should start. Lars, climb in with me on my signal. Jefferson, meet us at the bottom of the slope."

Once the car was in motion, Anne slipped into the car, motioning Lars to do the same. Then she began the process of starting the engine, muttering to herself, "Ignition, then starter." She pressed her foot down on the button at the floorboards and miraculously the car roared to a start.

Once at the bottom, Anne kept the car rev'd while Jefferson ran down to meet them.

They found Missy sitting on the ground, her skirts billowing out while two of the puppies wrestled on top of them. The mother dog, head resting on her forepaws, watched protectively until the motorcar approached. Then she leapt to her feet. Emitting a series of sharp barks, she moved between the car and the puppies.

Anne stopped the car, keeping a careful distance between the distraught dog, but close enough to talk to Missy. She motioned Lars and Jefferson out of the car.

Missy looked up and a smile lit her face. "You found a motorcar."

The dog looked at Missy in confusion.

"Settle down now. They're friends," Missy said, petting the dog, which sat with a show of reluctance. The dog glanced at Missy and then back at the motorcar as if to let her know Missy better know what she's doing.

"Yup," said Jefferson, acting like he had personally found the motorcar, fixed it, and brought it to Missy.

"Any problems while we were gone?" Anne asked.

"Nope," Missy said. "One nice couple stopped by and asked me what I was doing out this late, so I gave them a puppy."

"You gave them a puppy?" Jefferson asked.

"Everyone likes puppies," Missy replied, like a teacher stating a basic fact of life to her class's slowest student."

Jefferson scowled. "And that's it? They just left?"

"Yep. With their puppy." Missy turned to Lars. "Did you get some food? The dogs are really, really hungry, especially their mom."

Their mom, Lars noted, was looking pointedly at him. Apparently, she was getting over her fear of people, at least people with food.

"Yeah, when we searched the place looking for the amphora — back when we thought it was a normal sized vase, not something life-sized."

Missy held up her hand. "Wait. Life-sized?"

Lars motioned to the quilt-wrapped amphora in the back seat. "Life-sized. Can you believe it? Anyway, I had to search the icebox. Iceboxes," he added. "They had three. Rich folk like that, it never bothers me to help myself to some of their stuff."

Lars removed several strips of bacon from the butcher paper bundle in his right pocket and offered them to the dogs. The puppies ran right up and snatched a piece each, even the runt of the litter. Mom, though, approached cautiously and sniffed his hand and the bacon repeatedly, before grabbing a piece, retreating back to Missy, chewing and swallowing.

"So, you're friends now?" Lars asked Missy.

"Best friends," Missy confirmed, "but I don't know what to call her. We can't keep calling her 'mom.' We need to name the puppies, too."

"So, what have you thought of?"

"The puppies can wait, but their mother needs a name. She's real smart. Look how she watches us when we talk about her."

"Doggo?" Lars suggested. "Or Spot? Our dog back at the farm was named Spot."

"She doesn't have any spots," Jefferson pointed out. "Canis Cato, after the great man's dogs. Did you know that Romans used to train dogs to go into battle. They put spiked collars on them so enemies couldn't grab them. They were soldiers, just like any Roman legionnaire."

Missy shuddered. No one was sending her dogs into combat.

"What's the hold up?" Anne called from the car. "Get the dogs loaded and let's go."

"Missy says we need to name the mother dog first."

Anne tapped her head gently on the steering wheel, clearly exasperated. "Name the dog Duke and let's go."

"She's a mother dog. She can't be a duke," Missy protested.

Anne's tone was sharp, final, and had just an edge of a threat. "Duchess. Now Missy. Let's not get pinched by the police here. Local cops aren't known for being gentle."

Missy sighed and spoke gently to the dog, "Your name is Duchess now. Come on Duchess. Come on puppies." She hissed at Lars, "Give me the bacon. I'll use it to lure them into the motorcar."

They were finally all settled in the car. Missy and Lars in front, crammed into the front passenger seat. Jefferson, the puppies and the mother dog looking unsteady and suspicious were loaded in the back with the amphora.

Captain Anne revved the engine, pushing the car to get up to speed. It roared like a great beast and jerked forward.

That's when it happened.

Duchess stood up with several panicky barks. Her paws scraped for purchase, but all they found was the edge of the quilt. Her claws dug into the quilt and pulled it to the side.

Jefferson, who had been focused on Missy and Lars and not the dogs didn't notice until too late.

The back door popped open and the amphora, jerked to the side by the car's sudden lurching and accelerated by the startled scrambling of Duchess and her puppies, rolled from the car. It missed a nearby mud puddle that might have saved it and smashed onto the gravel path with a crash. One of the puppies tumbled and fell with it.

Duchess barked in panic, and her puppies joined her, raising a ruckus.

Anne stopped the car and all four of them stared at the quilts, which were previously shaped like a very large vase but were now crumpled on the ground covering the broken pieces of the vase. Next to them the puppy whined and then barked.

Duchess leapt from the car and tenderly grabbed the puppy in her jaws by the scruff of its neck.

Missy looked over the dog and exclaimed, "Thank heavens no one was hurt. The poor little thing just got a fright."

"The pot," Lar's voice came out in a croak. He swallowed and swallowed again.

"Amphora," Jefferson said.

"In pieces," Anne said, staring. "Pick it up, Jefferson and Lars. Put it in the car. Missy, get your dogs organized. We still need to get out of here."

The next morning, once back aboard the *Lightning Bug*, which had carried them a nice distance from Cairo to their relief, they assessed their score spread across the worn wooden deck. A broken pot, no car, a bunch of meat, and a few shiny trinkets.

Lars taking his turn as chef, passing out bowls of oatmeal, fresh blackberries, and thick slices of the ham they'd filched. They sprawled on the deck, eating, talking, and taking turns feeding scraps to the puppies. Unlike yesterday, Duchess now refused to take food from anyone's hand but Missy's.

"OK, hear me out," Jefferson began. "The amphora might be a dead loss, but…"

"Might be? Might be?" Lars said, sifting through the pieces still sitting on one of the quilts.

"OK. It is a dead loss." Jefferson picked up the old stone box they'd found in its wreckage. "But this looks like something special. It's very old," Jefferson said. He handed it to Lars who slid one of his picks along the box lid until he found the mechanism, then popped it. He groaned in disappointment. No jewels. No jewelry. Not even a set of old coins. Just an old scroll.

He handed it back to Jefferson who squinted at it. This is the real treasure," he said. "We can't unroll it, it will fracture. Look at it, though. It's ancient Greek."

Lars considered it. "You think the client knew about it?"

Anne looked at it and twirled a twist of hair as she thought. "If he did, he should have been honest with us. I suppose it's ours now. If we can find a buyer for something like this. Oscar?"

Oscar, whose little black book of contacts was legendary, nodded slowly. "I might be able to."

Anne glared at the pieces of clay, worthless now. "I guess we're taking a loss on this one. We took half down and now we can't deliver the amphora."

"It's not a loss," Missy said. "We rescued Duchess and her puppies. They might have died without us."

"Oh, we're great thieves," Jefferson said. "Famed in dogdom as a crack team of puppy emancipators."

"Cracking in Cairo," Lars jested as he helped himself to another thick piece of ham, only to have it stolen from his fingers by one of the puppies.

Missy laughed at his consternation. "Look at them thieving already. They're going to make top notch members of the crew."

PINCHED IN PEORIA

AUTHORS OF LIGHTNING SCARRED
C. S. STEIN

PINCHED IN PEORIA

A BARNACLES SHORT STORY

Pinched in Peoria: *We knew we wanted a story about a jail-break, but we didn't know which member of the team was going to be pinched and put in jail. That's when Sapphire stepped right up and introduced herself to us.*

PINCHED IN PEORIA

Sapphire, July 12, 1913, 1:00 pm

Sapphire had always wondered what it felt like to be in jail. Not enough to get herself arrested, of course, but the curiosity nonetheless itched at her as the prospect of new experiences often did.

Now she had her answer. Jail was as dull as yesterday's dishwater. Gray concrete walls, gray steel bars, and a graying, balding, potbellied sergeant doing paperwork on a small, dilapidated desk under an even smaller window that allowed only fragments of light to penetrate the dismal space. The place needed a woman's touch. And pillows. Lots of pillows. The wooden bench on which Sapphire sat was hard and uneven. It burrowed into her backside. The stained linoleum floor was cold and the air slightly chill. Sapphire was old enough to want a bit more comfort with her excitement these days.

Even having an entire theater troupe for company didn't make jail entertaining. They were crammed together, the women in her cell, the men in the adjacent cells on either side. It was more claustrophobic than the afternoon Sammy, her former husband, God rest his infernal soul, insisted on checking out a cave as a potential drop site for his latest load of illicit goods.

Next to her, the troupe's leading lady practically bounced through a series of pliés and then began a set of exercises. She happily explained she found them in a Physical Culture magazine someone left in the theater, Peoria's new Orpheum theater. That's where they'd all been arrested. She practically burbled. "Come on Sapphire! Weakness is a crime! It said so in the magazine. Don't be a criminal."

"We're in jail," Sapphire replied. "Obviously we're criminals." She fingered through her hair again, doing her best to get it to lay flat.

"We're not criminals. We're actors. A little jail time is good for our careers. It's good publicity. Our next performance will probably sell out."

"Only if we can get out of jail," Ken Rockford said from the neighboring cell. He banged his fist against its bars. "How can this have happened? We weren't even banned in Boston. Arrested in fricking Peoria? Who gets arrested for indecency in Peoria? The whole damn city is indecent. Locals call it Roaring Peoria. How can it be roaring if the cops lock folks up on trumped up indecency charges?"

The balding police guard responded in kind, pounding his fist on the much-scarred top of his desk. "Hey! Stop flapping your gums and mind your language. That's my city you're talking about. I walked a beat when Teddy Roosevelt himself said Peoria's main street was the world's most beautiful drive. We don't need you theater people cluttering up our streets or talking bad about our city."

The sweet smell of roses and river weeds wafted into the room and drew Sapphire's attention to the door through which a woman entered.

Hot tar and damnation! If that wasn't Annie Harris walking into the jail as cool as nobody's business and dressed in her Sunday best, like any dowager out for a stroll through the jail cells. Sapphire had to hand it to her. When Annie did the legit look, she did it well.

"Officer, I'm told you have a friend of mine here."

No Annie! Sapphire caught her eye and shook her head.

The guard ran his eyes up and down Annie's slight frame and strict schoolmarm demeanor. She'd gathered her hair and pinned it up tightly, complementing the look with a jaunty straw hat with an enormous blue striped silk bow. "You friends with one of the so-called actors?"

Annie laughed, but her eyes darted around the room taking in the cells, their occupants, and everything else. "Actors? What are actors doing in jail?"

"Indecent exposure, I think. I weren't there. I heard they was carrying on in public. Lots of witnesses. At the Orpheum Theater, no less. Biggest theater in the city. Still practically new. It just opened two years ago in 1911, my last year walking a beat. These so-called actors were carrying on in there like it's a brothel in the Merry-Go-Round." He paused and added "proper lady like you wouldn't know about that part of town." Ken Rockford banged the cell door again, clattering it loudly. "We were framed. They say we didn't pay into the Policeman's Protective Union Fund. This doesn't even happen in damned Memphis. It shouldn't happen anywhere along the bloody Orpheum Circuit, even in godforsaken Peoria with its shiny, new theater."

"I told you once to stop flapping your gums. Now I'm telling you again. Look what you've done. This fine lady is shocked by your language. Shocked. Now shut your yap or you'll be in a world of hurt."

Sapphire could see Annie was trying to look shocked, though not particularly well. Her best friend could use some acting lessons. Once they were back aboard the *Lightning Bug*, their houseboat home, Sapphire would take that on. Or maybe one of the actors could give Annie a few tips. Meanwhile, though, she had to get out of jail without the authorities connecting her to Annie or Oscar or the other Barnacles aboard the *Lightning Bug* or learning about Sapphire's checkered past. She also needed to free the sweet bit of heaven who'd been kissing her in the theater's wings before the police raided it. She looked over to the adjoining cell and winked at him.

He knelt on one knee, his hands clasped before his chest, and gazed soulfully at her. His eyes looked like they'd been crafted by Aphrodite herself for the sole purpose of seducing women. She blew him a kiss, which he mock caught and clasped to his heart.

One year grifting tourists in Atlantic City. Eight years married to the Newark mob. Two years running the rivers with the Barnacles, a happy, go-lucky bunch of thieves. In all that time did she get jugged?

No.

But kiss an actor and suddenly she's cooling her tail in jail. The devil was having fun at her expense. Annie would too once she got out of this joint and they were alone.

Annie smiled sweetly at the guard. "I must have been misinformed. I don't see my friend. I don't know how I could have fallen for that prank. No friend of mine gets arrested and locked up in jail. Besides, my friends don't fall all over actors like a ton of bricks. It's bad luck. And in very poor taste."

Oscar, July 12, 1913, 5:30 pm

Samson's Steakhouse was clicking right along. Gentlemen in top hats and black homburgs escorted ladies in the latest fashions, shining with beads and sporting colorful, fancy feathers to tables set in make-believe grottos.

Oscar had been lucky to get a table. It was near the kitchen, barely big enough for him, Annie, and the contact. If Annie showed, which was always the question.

An older woman with a proud bearing and a hawk-like nose sauntered to his table. Her clothes were less colorful but better cut than those around her.

Oscar scrambled to his feet.

"Mr. Little, I presume?" she said, her voice just a bit rough with age or dryness.

Oscar sketched a bow. "Madame, you have me at a disadvantage. I wasn't given your name."

A smile creaked across her aged face. "As it should be."

Oscar nodded and pulled out her chair. "What shall I call you, Madame?"

She braced her hands against the table briefly and sat down slowly, moving like a mechanical doll needing oil. "Madame is sufficient for now. I understand you are having a problem with the local constabulary?"

"Not us, precisely. A friend."

The waiter arrived and without a word set two glasses and a bottle of whiskey by Madame and then left discreetly. Clearly, she was a regular. She poured a finger of whiskey for herself and motioned the question to him. He nodded, and she poured a bit of whiskey for him and slid the glass toward him.

It was strong and smoky, something from the local distillery that claimed to be the largest in the world. It wasn't to Oscar's taste, but he believed in letting the contact set the tone for the meetings. It made things so much simpler to be easy-going at first.

Madame waved her hand. "It's always for a friend, isn't it? Tell me what happened."

And so, Oscar described what he knew of Sapphire's situation. When he finished, Madame's eyes glinted. "You want to get the actors released, do you?"

"My friend, who may not be an actor."

"Why not just pay off the police? Everyone knows actors playing Peoria have to pay off local officials. Practically anyone passing through town on business does. It's no different than paying off the mob in Chicago or both cops and mobsters in New York. Peoria's mayor has quite a racket. Everyone pays. Even gamblers and Merry-Go-Round streetwalkers. The mayor's racket keeps all the other rackets in line. One hand washes the other, you understand."

"The lady joining us will have an opinion on that. But let's say she nixes the idea. How can you help us get our friend out?"

"Well, I can give you a few ideas. What you make of them is up to you. If you ask me, paying off the cops would be much easier."

Anne arrived a few minutes later, just as Madame drained her whiskey glass. Anne wore a fashionable dress and a large straw hat. She fit in perfectly with the restaurant's customers, though Oscar suspected this was happenstance.

Oscar rose as she arrived. A waiter appeared, placed a glass for her, and pulled out her chair, departing after she seated herself.

Madame watched, her sharp eyes missing nothing that passed between Anne and Oscar. She was the first to speak. "Miss Harris, your agent asks for our help. You can do this the easy way or the difficult way."

Annie sat upright in her chair with the perfect posture of a woman raised in the upper class and accustomed to fussy dresses and corsets. She took off her gloves slowly and laid them in her lap. Oscar realized Annie was stalling for some reason. To think, perhaps? Finally, she said, "I'm inclined toward easy. Let's discuss that first."

Madame inclined her head, a slight grin on her face. "A woman after my own heart. Very well. As I explained to Mr. Little here, the mayor runs Peoria like a prize mule. The mule pulls his wagon, or he beats it until it does. Anyone who wants to do business in Peoria pays him off. Even actors."

Annie pressed her lips together and then briefly shook her head. "We don't pay people extra to do their jobs. Civil servants work for the people. The mayor is no different."

"Even if paying will be both cheaper and safer?"

"Even then. It's a matter of principle. Start paying them and the next thing you know you don't have a decent city anymore."

"There are some that say that Peoria isn't a decent city. It didn't get its nickname by accident." Madame's eyes glinted but her mirth didn't reach her lips.

Annie didn't respond, merely flagged down the waiter and asked for a cup of hot tea. She took a few sips in the ensuing silence. Oscar loved these moments in negotiation when debate and dickering transitioned to silence and significant looks. The trick was not to break the quiet. He took a sip of the smoky whiskey holding it in his mouth for a moment before letting it burn down his throat.

Madame spoke first. "There is another way, but it will cost you. And it's something of a good deed. Depends on the type of people you are."

"Tell me," Annie said.

Jefferson, July 12, 1913, 6:30 pm

The briefing started the minute Annie and Oscar returned to the *Lightning Bug*, their home and getaway vehicle now quietly tied up at a pier. With all of them on the top deck it sometimes got a bit loud for Jefferson, who preferred the quiet cabin he shared with Lars to all the chit chat.

Jefferson pressed his palms together and extended his fingers, enjoying the feeling as he stretched each to its limit and the knuckles popped. Annie had said to be ready just in case. For Jefferson that meant that somewhere a safe needed to be cracked or a lock sweet-talked until it opened for him. He couldn't wait.

Lars looked as eager as a puppy. "How does it look in there? Did you talk to Sapphire?"

Annie gave them the rundown brisk and clean. "Didn't talk to her. Only one door into the cellblock, but the guard is old and bored. Cheap locks on the cell doors that Jefferson could probably pick one-handed. Barred windows in the cells, but an unbarred window near the guard's desk. Lars could squeeze through it. Long corridor leading away from the cells. Don't know what's back there. Maybe more cells."

"Maybe another entrance," Lars suggested. "Or at least a window without a guard under it."

They hadn't planned to do a job in Peoria. Probably no criminal enterprise does, Jefferson mused. It's not like thieves are on the Orpheum circuit. They weren't vaudevillians like those locked up with Sapphire who needed to discover if their act "plays in Peoria" before taking it to Chicago or New York.

No, he and his fellow Barnacles, the nickname they'd given themselves, were just run-of-the-mill thieves. Well, more like run-of-the-river thieves.

Jefferson laughed at his private joke causing Lars to look at him quizzically. Annie stopped her briefing momentarily.

"Something you want to add, Jefferson?"

"No, Ma'am. Just a stray thought. I'm listening." "See that you do."

Lars said, "I could scale the police station tonight, get into the cells through the window you mentioned."

"And what?" Annie asked. "Climbing things is not a plan. There's the guard to deal with, and I don't think Sapphire's as eager as you to climb down the side of a police station."

Jefferson's thoughts drifted down the river as Lars and Annie went at it like usual. Lars always wanted to climb, the higher and harder the better. He tried to arrange half their missions around some spectacular climb or similar derring-do. Annie wasn't having any of it this time.

Jefferson considered Sapphire's arrest. The Barnacles were pretty good thieves, at least when it came to avoiding cops and jails. Scout the job, do the job, and then float down the river— the Illinois or Ohio or Mississippi. Whatever river was handy.

On the rivers, the *Lightning Bug*, intermingled with barges laden with coal and grain, steamboats carrying passengers and tourists, assorted fishing and pleasure craft, and the occasional fellow houseboat. No one paid any attention to them, just another down-on-their-luck family traveling the river, eking out a living and looking for work. They never did a job in the same city twice, at least not in the same year, and they kept on the move, avoiding cops and marks and anyone else harboring unreasonable animus against them.

That's why Jefferson and his fellow Barnacles were surprised when Sapphire got herself pinched—in Peoria of all places.

Sapphire was probably surprised, too, but she hadn't had a chance to communicate that to her partners in crime since her pinching. Not even during Anne's brief visit to reconnoiter the jail. Now they had to get Sapphire unpinched, back aboard the *Lightning Bug,* and out of Peoria.

He turned his attention back to the conversation. Apparently, Lars had convinced Captain Anne and they were discussing the logistics of the climb.

Lars, July 12, 1913, 8:15 pm

Lars felt the familiar buoyancy flooding his veins as he pulled himself up the side of the police station. While he'd learned to climb by climbing mountains, nothing compared to the double thrill of being high off the ground under his own power and having to avoid notice. All of his senses were on alert as he listened to the song of the night, a bustle of voices, horses pulling carts and wagons, and the occasional automobile.

He'd managed to convince Annie to let him do what he did best: climb. He would make the most of it. And maybe Sapphire would want to try rappelling down the side of the building. It could be fun.

He placed his fingers carefully, blessing the town elders who'd decided on a mix of rough brick and stone for the police station. Its uneven facade presented lots of interesting handholds for an enterprising cat burglar. Lars clung to the shadows as he moved up.

He spidered a finger up the wall, and felt it sink into slime that had gathered between the stones. He wiped his hand on the brick and probed carefully to the side until he found a dry spot.

Securing his grip, he reached for the next hold, and then the next. It was an easy climb, easier than he expected. As he moved his right foot into a crevice recently vacated by his hand, he heard a shout from below and froze in that awkward position, his right knee almost pressed to his face as he clung to the wall.

Had someone seen him?

He'd carefully dressed to match the brick of the building, but there was always a chance someone with sharp eyes had looked up at just the right time and spotted him, particularly since it was still daylight. He took a breath and tried to blend into the wall. Nothing to see here. He hoped Jefferson was having an easier time.

Jefferson, July 12, 1913, 8:30 pm

Jefferson heard voices as he moved quietly toward the cells. Lars had proved correct. The corridor Anne had seen ran the length of the cell block floor. As dusk arrived, Lars helped him shimmy up a drainpipe and pry open a window. He placed his feet carefully on the scuffed linoleum floor as he tiptoed down the shadowed, unlit corridor, not making a sound.

Someone else, though, was making plenty of noise. Several someone elses, he realized as he neared the well-lit cellblock. The unmistakable odors of cheap cigars and somewhat better whiskey joined the cacophony of voices echoing down the corridor toward him.

"I'll call," said a gruff male voice.

"Raise ten," said another, followed by the tinkling sound of clay poker chips.

Jefferson stopped. What sort of jail handed out cards, booze, and cigars? Even in "Roarin' Peoria," there were prohibition activists, fussy women's virtue campaigners who worked to close bars and shut down the local red-light district, the Merry-Go-Round. They certainly wouldn't approve of jailbirds drinking, gambling, and smoking. Bless them! If this caught on, convicts would leave prison so skilled with cards, few cardsharps would stand a chance against them. Crime paid best when virtue kept competition small.

"He's bluffing. He's got a pair of twos and nothing else," came another voice, this one from the direction of the cells. An outraged cry of "no, I don't! I got plenty!" quickly followed. Jefferson tucked himself against the wall as tightly as he could and peered around the doorframe. A skinny civilian and three uniformed cops, two younger and one older, overweight, and balding, sat around the desk, which they'd turned into an

ersatz card table by placing a wide board over it.

Dressed in a striped shirt with a high collar and wearing fussy-looking pince-nez glasses, the civilian periodically fondled the large pile of chips in front of him.

Not hard to tell who was having a good night, and who wasn't. The outraged cop was down to his last few chips. The other young cop wasn't doing much better. Overweight and balding looked like he was holding his own. He matched Anne's description of the only guard on duty.

One of the prisoners, an older man with a peeved look, had shouted out the outraged guard's hand. Jefferson couldn't tell from his angle whether it was truth or lie, but that didn't matter to the poker players.

The old guard, eyes narrowed in anger, growled. "I told you to shut your yap. You've been getting on my nerves all day. Now you're going to see how much worse it can get for you."

The prisoner sighed dramatically. "We are wrongly imprisoned. Pining in durance vile. Waiting for truth to triumph over wickedness. We amuse ourselves as best we can. If our meager amusements do not meet with your approval, release us. I'm the director of our little troupe. I'll ensure that each of you esteemed gentlemen get comped tickets."

Jefferson consulted his memory and realized that this must be the director, Ken Rockford. Annie counted him as an asset, though Jefferson couldn't see why.

"Close your yap!"

The prisoner continued as if he hadn't been interrupted. "For you and your dates. At the best show in town. Front seats at the Orpheum. Sixteen hundred seats in the theater and you and your dates would be in the best."

Some woman in the middle cell yelled "Just leave it be, Ken. Or pay them the dough. Whatever it takes. I can't take this anymore. It's worse than that gig in Omaha."

The outraged cop threw down his cards, snuffed out his cigar stub, and stomped over to the cell. He opened its door, which groaned on old hinges, grabbed Ken Rockford, and pulled him out. Swift as butter, he cuffed Ken's wrists behind his back and banged him hard against the bars and then again for good measure.

Jefferson winced in sympathy.

"You need to shut your yap. I can't have you yellin' your nonsense when my luck is about to change. So, shut up or else."

"Or else what?" If it was possible to strike a dramatic pose in handcuffs, Ken Rockford was trying.

Jefferson turned his gaze to the wall. He didn't want to watch. Besides, he wasn't here for the show. He was here to get Sapphire out. That would have been hard with one guard to outmaneuver. It now seemed impossible with four in the room. Would their distraction get all four of them to leave the room long enough for him to get Sapphire out?

As if she heard his thoughts, Sapphire took that moment to make trouble.

Sapphire stood up and strode to the cell bars. "Hey! Hey!" she said as she leaned against the bars and smiled sweetly, her face the picture of innocence. "I'm not saying that Ken's not a pill, but you can't let him get to you. What do you say about giving us a break?"

"I hate actors," one of the cops at the table said and tossed down his cards. "Give me a thief or a fancy moll any day and twice on Sunday."

"How long do we need to keep 'em?" asked the cop holding Ken.

"Chief didn't say," replied old and balding. "He was in the audience. I guess they made him good and mad."

"Not hard to see how."

Jefferson silently agreed. Would Ken cause trouble for him when he made his move to free Sapphire? He checked his pocket watch. Five more minutes until Lars would be in position, assuming he wasn't delayed. He needed to bide his time.

Sapphire, July 18, 1913, 8:40 pm

Someone shouted down on the street outside the jail.

Sapphire walked to the wall with the window and stood on her toes to peer out and down toward the street. She couldn't stand being trapped like this, crammed into a too small space uglier than the worst dressing room she'd ever had to stand in.

Even her cramped quarters on the *Lightning Bug* were better than this, though of course she'd decorated those herself.

Also, the cops' cigar smoke was getting to her, bringing up memories of Sammy, God rest his infernal soul. Their last night together before the hit had been explosive. She shuddered. He'd been self-satisfied and so possessive after killing her lover. Damn him! And damn the sex for being so good. Sammy had been better than any actor.

Living with Sammy she'd felt like a songbird in a golden cage. By contrast, being locked in jail felt more like being a poor little mink trapped in a too-tight box ready to become a coat. Or a stole. She stroked her shoulder where her mink stole used to sit and sighed. That life was gone.

Good riddance.

The Bank Street mob had freed Sapphire from Sammy, then she'd freed herself from the whole Newark mafia. Now she needed to free herself from this jail. No one kept Sapphire in a cage. At least not for long.

She'd examined the locks on the cell doors earlier. Cheap, but large and heavy. She lacked the tools and skill to pick them. Pretending to examine the street below, she surreptitiously tested the bars over the window. The cops were still arguing over their card game and what to do to poor, big-mouthed Ken.

No rust and all the bars seemed well-set.

Outside an older woman and a young girl who looked to be about 17 were walking down the street, arguing.

"Hey! Come here!"

They turned to the jail and the younger one blanched, pointing up.

Lars, July 18, 1913, 8:45 pm

Lars continued his climb, moving up the face of the police station where the shadow cast by a nearby building helped conceal him. The brickwork became less even as he climbed, and handholds were easier to find. He relaxed into the repetitive series of movements.

Right hand, right foot. Left hand, left foot. Repeat.

As he neared the station's upper floor, where Anne said Sapphire and her actor friends were being held, he had to edge out of the shadow and toward the window he and Jefferson had spotted from the ground. There weren't any bars on it, but they had no idea where it led, or how easy it would be to open while clinging to the side of the building.

He paused, took several deep breaths, and began edging to his right slowly, a few inches at a time to be certain of his grip. As he neared the window, he heard a loud scream coming from the ground below.

"The prisoners! They're escaping! Mad murderers walking amongst us. Help! Oh Help!"

Jeez! It was an old woman who'd been arguing on the street earlier. In a desperate maneuver, Lars dove through the window. He barely missed hitting a guard, landed on the edge of a board laid atop an old desk, and scattered the cards and chips of what looked like a lively poker game across the room.

"I had the winning hand! This is just not right," said one of the cops sounding aggrieved.

It was perhaps not the moment to ask to join in. Lars saw Jefferson do a smooth run to the cell doors, banking on the distraction, holding a set of keys he must have lifted.

There was supposed to be just one guard, Lars thought. Instead, three uniformed cops and another in a fancy suit were drawing roscoes, which they pointed in his direction.

This wasn't good. As a professional thief he disliked guns, particularly in the hands of unreliable people. Like cops.

He lifted his hands. "Don't shoot. I'm just visiting."

The largest cop growled, "Yeah, and it's going to be a nice long visit." He turned to the other two. "Put them in the lower cells."

"But you said we don't use them anymore. Chief needs them for..."

"Do what I tell you. Put these two downstairs." He gestured at Lars and Jefferson. Then he swung around to face the cells and waved his gun in what Lars was pretty sure was a violation of safe firearm practice. "In fact, put all of them below. I'm sick of their shenanigans."

"All of them? Women, too?"

"Nah. Leave the women up here. At least they're decorative. And quiet."

Jefferson, Lars, and assorted actors were poked and pushed to walk down a set of old cement stairs until they arrived at a small, dark basement. One of the guards pulled out his flashlight. Its beam illuminated two small cells with iron bars and a rough, dirty cement floor. The entire place smelled disgusting, like Uncle Jim's pig pens, Lars thought.

The guards locked them in the far cell and returned to the upper floor to escort the remaining actors down to these basement cells. Lars and Jefferson felt around the walls until they found the false one Anne described. Lars released its latch and pulled out the expected notebook, which Jefferson quickly grabbed. "I need to decipher the code," he said.

As Jefferson worked, Lars sat back to wait. The guards returned with the remaining actors, locked them in the cell opposite theirs, and departed without noticing Jefferson who quickly hid and then retrieved the notebook as their footsteps departed. It was just a waiting game from here out.

If Annie was right, they'd be released tomorrow. If she was wrong, they'd need to plan another jailbreak, this time from the basement's reeking cells. Had something died down here?

Oscar July 18, 1913, 10:00 pm

It was well past visiting hours, but with the help of one of Madame's friends, the cops allowed Oscar into the jail to talk to Ken Rockford. The basement cells looked like they hadn't been cleaned since the Civil War. For all he knew they hadn't. Old locks, spots of rust on the bars, and smears of who knew what growing on some of the walls. Oscar wrinkled his nose in disgust. He couldn't identify the smell, but it was the worst smelling jail he'd ever been in.

Not that he made a habit of visiting jails.

The male prisoners had been moved down here along with the two rapscallions who'd tried to break them out, the guard explained. They wouldn't see the light of day for a long time, if ever, he assured Oscar.

As Oscar entered, several of the actors made a fuss. He came close to the bars ostensibly to confer with Ken Rockford, the director. "Sir, I am doing everything possible to help you."

"Are you a lawyer?" Rockford demanded.

Oscar drew himself up and made a show of brushing dust off his borrowed coat. "I, sir, am the law clerk." He angled his body carefully to obscure his movements, continuing his conversation with Rockford.

"Now explain to me why you were arrested."

While Rockford began a long and whining story, Oscar felt the feather touch of a hand slipping something into his pocket. Had he not expected it, he would have been hard-pressed to notice it. Once again, he marveled at Jefferson's skill. Or maybe it was Lars. He couldn't take the risk of looking. The object passed to him was large, hopefully the notebook and not some scrawled excuse. He finished his conversation with Rockford and left as quickly with an apologetic look toward the imprisoned men.

"I must protest their treatment," Oscar said to the guard as they climbed the stairs leading to the main prison. "I wouldn't store pigs in those cells, much less men."

"Shows what you know," the guard replied. "The chief used to store his prize pigs in those very cells. If they're good enough for pigs, they're good enough for actors. You'd think so too if you had to spend time with them."

Sapphire, July 18, 1913, 7:30 pm

Sapphire breathed in the familiar smell of the theater and actor sweat permeating the theater just before the curtain rose on the Friday night performance. It smelled like hope and passion. Not to mention strong young actors, like Nicholas who'd pulled her into his arms in the crevice behind the curtains to lay one on her a week ago, landing her in jail.

The audience rumbled, like a beast all around her, excited to see the first full performance of the "Performance Banned in Peoria." She suspected some members of the audience were hoping for another raid. She chuckled to herself. Oscar's contact had kept her word. They'd been released the next day with many effusive apologies.

The Orpheum hadn't stinted when it came to building their new theater. It was a grand and beautiful spectacle, with intricate architecture and colorful frescoes. Everything was new and gleamed, from the gold flecked wallpaper to the deep purple velvet curtains to the new electric chandeliers that sent glimmers of light across the theater.

Ken really had come through with tickets for the Barnacles. Decent seats, too. Plus, Oscar had applied some pressure to get box seats for Madame and her granddaughter who was just seventeen and glowed with the radiance God graced youth. They must have settled the argument they'd been having on the street because they smiled happily at each other.

The girl was dressed in the height of the latest fashion, opulent white lace bodice, just a little daring for her age, and a long white columnar dress caught up below her breasts. She seemed quite taken by her first experience in the theater, waving her handkerchief at the actors as they appeared on stage.

Jefferson pointed up at their box and elbowed Sapphire. "Look!"

"Hey! Don't point at them. They'll see." Sapphire pulled his arm down. "Don't you know how to behave in the theater?"

"Oh. Sorry. Do you think that's the girl in the notebook?"
"The girl in the notebook?"

"Yeah. The notebook we pinched in the basement cells. It was a doozy. I read a few pages and it was like something from a dime novel."

"Was it her diary?"

"Maybe. If so, she's had a rum life." Jefferson thought for a moment and then shook his head. "Nah! I don't think so."

"Why not?"

"It read like a novel. No girl or woman could imagine things like that, much less participate. Look at her. Pretty as a rose and innocent as a daisy. Must be someone else's story."

A man joined the two women in their box. Was that Mr. Singleton of Singleton & Sons Publishing? Sapphire met him once in New York. Sapphire turned away, hoping he wouldn't recognize her. She didn't need anything getting back to the Newark mob about her location.

As she did, Sapphire smiled to herself. That girl would do just fine. No wonder the notebook read like a dime novel. It was one. Or would be once Singleton published it.

The lights dimmed and the curtain opened to reveal the grand living room in a posh house. The audience hushed as the actors took their places. Sapphire's heart swelled in her chest. The great romance began again, as it did every Friday and Saturday night on the Orpheum Circuit. As it always did, the theater renewed Sapphire's faith in love and life. For to-night at least.

Tomorrow they'd get back on the *Lightning Bug* and sail down-river to their next job. But tonight? Magic. Sapphire breathed it in. Better than church incense or the smell of good champagne. It was transformation made visible.

CHICAGO SMOKE

AUTHORS OF LIGHTNING SCARRED
C. S. STEIN
CHICAGO SMOKE
A BARNACLES SHORT STORY

Chicago Smoke: *It's never a good thing when things suddenly explode, especially when Jefferson is trying to concentrate on opening a safe. It all goes south from there.*

CHICAGO SMOKE

Jefferson delicately manipulated the safe's third tumbler into place and began the slow process of determining the fourth and last. As he slowly twisted the dial, listening carefully, the building rocked violently. His hand slipped from the dial, twirling it, and undoing 20 minutes of work.

A loud boom followed, accompanied by the sound of tinkling glass and the assorted thuds and crunchings of numerous falling objects. "What the hell was that?"

Screams from the street below rent the quiet night.

"Something that's going to draw the police to this neighborhood. Hurry, Jefferson," said Anne, their nominal leader.

Jefferson, Anne, and their fellow Barnacles were on the fifth floor of what used to be a bank. It was an office building now. Well, offices on the upper floors. A deli, grocer, and other shops occupied the ground floor, the high arched windows of the former bank converted to doorways. The bank's marble floors and high vaulted ceiling, though, remained. A wide central staircase led from the bank's former lobby to the second floor, once executive offices, now apartments. The Barnacles avoided that stairway. It ended at the second floor, and there were "too many eyes there." So, they'd climbed one of the long stairways on either end of the tall building. Those led to every floor and the roof.

The safe was in the backroom of an office that occupied half the fifth floor. Jefferson resumed trying to crack it. For a moment, he thought he smelled smoke. The power of suggestion, probably. They were too high for smoke from the street to reach them. His partners in crime, the Barnacles, were in the outer office. He tried to concentrate through their chatter and returned to working on the safe.

"An earthquake?" asked Missy.

"In Chicago?" said Oscar. "That seems unlikely. Chicago isn't on a fault line."

"It's possible," said Jefferson, unable to avoid the temptation to correct their self-styled scientist. "There was a huge earthquake south of here in Missouri. It was a century ago."

"Maybe, but that sounded more like an explosion. Unless earthquakes go 'boom,'" Oscar said.

"Sometimes," Jefferson said, though he wasn't precisely sure that was true, never having been in an earthquake before.

"Whatever it was," said Anne, "Michigan Avenue is just a couple blocks away. It's crawling with cops thanks to all the banks and ritzy businesses there. They'll be here in no time. This job is wrecked. Grab your gear. We're getting out of here."

"Where's Sapphire?" Lars asked.

"She went down Jackson Street after getting us past the guard and into this building," Oscar said. "She wanted to grab a quick drink before returning to the *Lightning Bug*. She's looking real sharp after the new paint job. The *Bug*," he clarified, "not Sapphire.

"Prettiest houseboat at the pier," Lars agreed.

Perhaps thinking he might have offended Sapphire even though she wasn't there, Oscar added "Sapphire looks good, too. Always nicely turned out, no matter the job. I hope she's OK. She should be well clear of whatever's going on in the street."

The building shook again, followed quickly by the boom of another explosion. Moments later, a strange smell wafted in, something acrid and sharp that burned the eyes.

Missy went to the window, and Jefferson heard her open the draperies. "Oscar? This looks bad." Her voice wavered. "I think this explosion was closer, and on this side of the building."

Oscar, Lars, and Anne joined Missy at the window. She was looking down and pointing at something. Flames in the street below turned the lights of the city red and wavering.

Jefferson glanced, couldn't see what they were looking at, and refocused his attention on the safe. He took a few deep breaths, blinked his eyes, and wiggled his fingers to release the tension. The key to any successful safecracking was limber fingers and an agile mind. The safe was a large model. It occupied almost half the wall of the office's storage room and was taller than Jefferson. It was probably original to the building, installed when it was built as a bank. Or perhaps the bank was built around it. That was a long time ago, though. The building had been carved into individual offices and stores when the bank failed 20 years ago in the panic of 1893.

Regardless, the building was conveniently near Lake Michigan, so they could quickly get back to the marina and aboard the *Lightning Bug,* their houseboat home and getaway vehicle. Then they'd slip out of town on the lake and head down the Illinois River, avoiding the local constabulary, who rarely took to the water. They seemed to have an aversion to it. Living on the *Bug* and escaping by water were central to the Barnacles' criminal exploits.

"Do you smell smoke?" asked Missy.

"No," Oscar said. "Wait," he sniffed. "Maybe,"

Jefferson remembered the first two numbers of the safe's combination and had a sense for where the third sat on the dial. That left only the fourth tumbler. If he worked fast, he could crack the safe in a few minutes. They'd grab the paintings their client wanted and take whatever other temptations the safe offered for themselves. Then they'd make their getaway, avoiding the commotion in the street below that occupied his companions' attention.

Their excited voices reverberated off the windows, seeming almost as loud as the first explosion. Thieves were supposed to be quiet—at least when they were on a job. He could work a lot quicker if they'd just stop talking about whatever was going on outside.

The others milled around, talking over one another excitedly. Didn't they realize that safecracking required a certain amount of quiet? The moments Jefferson spent with a safe were sacred, like being in church. People should talk in whispers. Not carouse as if they were at a damned tavern.

"All the windows I can see are closed," Anne said. "Any smoke must be coming from inside this building."

"Maybe it's drifting in from a lower floor window," Missy said, ever hopeful.

"Who would want to bomb this building?" Oscar asked. "We're nowhere near the Mercantile Exchange. There's nothing worth blowing up near here. This is just an old office building. Deli, laundromat, and grocery on the ground floor, apartments on the second floor, and accountants, a doctor, and low-rent lawyers on the upper floors. That's why our mark kept his stash here. He's the only one on this floor and he blended in with the other shysters."

Anne sniffed the air. "Worth blowing up or not, I definitely smell smoke now. It's time for us to go. That means you, too, Jefferson," she added after noticing he was still working on the safe. "Nothing in that safe is worth being blown up or burned alive."

"Just a minute," said Jefferson. "I almost have the last tumbler."

"Hey, I can see the smoke now," Lars called. "Look out the door. There's smoke in the hallway."

"Yeah," Oscar said, "it looks like it's coming up the stairway."

"There's hardly any, though," Missy said, joining them. "Just little wisps. That's good right?"

"We're on the fifth floor," said Oscar. "Smoke reaching us this quickly is almost definitely not good."

"Yeah, and it's thickening fast," said Anne. "We need to check the other staircase to see if it's clear. Go take a look, Missy."

Jefferson, though, stuck to his task. He heard Missy leave. Her steps echoed down the hallway as she walked to the hallway's far end. Jefferson continued to slowly twist the safe's dial, listening carefully. As Missy's footsteps faded, Jefferson felt Anne looming over him. She inhaled deeply and was about to speak when the fourth tumbler clicked into place, and Jefferson called "got it." He pulled the handle and the safe's heavy door creaked open with a puff of dust.

Anne stepped up beside Jefferson and peered in with him. The tall safe was stuffed with dozens of wooden crates and cardboard boxes in varying sizes and conditions. To their left and right were stacks and stacks of papers that never made it into the boxes or the filing cabinets lining the safe's right wall behind them or the shelves on the safe's left. Layers of dust, which increased in depth as he stared toward the back of the safe trying to figure out how to pull out what they needed, coated the piles' upper layers.

"It's stuffed to the gills," Anne said. "We don't have time to go through everything. Do you see them?"

"Can't see what's on the lower shelves without moving some boxes. If the paintings are framed, they could be in any of these big boxes. If the shyster cut them out of the frames, they could be rolled up like those." Jefferson pointed to the top shelf where several dozen large bundles of rolled papers sat. Arranged lengthwise, they jutted out from the narrow shelf and appeared ready to topple. "Some of the longer rolls look like they're the right size."

"Or they could be this building's architectural plans or some child's scribblings or something to do with any of the lawyer's cases. We can't sort through and unroll each one. There must be a hundred of them."

"I just got the safe open. We can't just leave all this loot."

"How can you tell the loot from the junk? It looks like the guy locked up everything he owned in here. There's half a sandwich on top of that cabinet in the corner," she pointed to a sandwich mummified and covered in dust. "And this," she said, reaching atop the closest stack of papers, "is an old bill." She blew the dust off it and glanced. "It's for heating coal of all things. It's a dozen years old, from before they converted this building to electricity."

"There's gotta be something worth taking," Jefferson said. He slanted his body and maneuvered carefully through the narrow spots between the piled boxes and began rummaging. "We're not going to get a second chance at this. All this goes up in smoke if the fire spreads, or the fire department will turn it into wet pulp if they get hoses up here."

"They've just arrived," Missy said, as she returned from her reconnaissance and stepped back into the office. "A fire engine just pulled up. Cops have closed off the street and the smoke's getting worse. It's not as bad in the far stairway, but you can smell it there, too. I heard lots of folks running down those stairs. So, the stairs must be safe, at least for now."

"Or people are too panicked to be careful and check," Anne said.

Missy walked to the safe and Oscar joined her, peering in over Anne's shoulder. "Where are the canvases?"

"Hey," replied Jefferson over his shoulder. He opened another box, grunted, tossed it aside, and opened another. "It's not like anything in here's labeled. Get in here and help. Start checking the big rolled papers on my left. Some of them look like they could be canvas or parchment."

"You heard Missy," Oscar said. "The smoke's getting worse. We need to leave soon, while there's still a chance of getting down the far staircase. Unless, of course, you like the idea of asphyxiating."

"It can take ten minutes to asphyxiate from smoke. And it's not even smoky here yet."

"Yet." Anne said.

"But we can't leave the canvases behind," Missy said. "They're someone's life's work."

"An obscure artist only our client cares about."

"Art is art. It matters. It mattered to the artist back when he painted them, and it matters to our client now."

"Then let's grab them all and get moving."

"And the cops? It's not like we can fold up the paintings and stick them in our pockets."

"One problem at a time," said Anne. "Right now let's avoid getting burned alive."

"Or crushed," Oscar added, "if this old building collapses."

"Get a sack. Maybe three sacks," said Jefferson. "Grab all the rolled papers. They're all potential paintings. That's our best bet. I've checked the larger boxes. No paintings, just a little cash and some coins and cheap jewelry, which I grabbed." He jingled his pockets. "We can sort through it later."

Oscar produced several sacks from his own copious jacket pockets, which the five Barnacles quickly filled. As they finished, wisps of foul-smelling smoke mixed with the safe's stale air.

Jefferson pushed the heavy door closed as they exited. "Just in case they get the fire out and we get a second chance," he said.

Smoke filled the hallway as they left the office. Jefferson wrapped his handkerchief over his nose and mouth. Oscar did the same with his and handed his spare to Lars. Anne pulled a scarf from her purse and handed another to Missy, which they wrapped around their faces as they rushed toward the stairs. Jefferson, Lars, and Oscar each carried a bulging sack of rolled papers. Cash and assorted miscellaneous loot, anything small and shiny, filled pockets and purses.

"This way," Missy said. "The far stairway wasn't too bad when I checked."

They walked quickly, Lars in the lead.

"Will the smoke damage the paintings?" Missy asked.

"Not as much as if we left them behind. But yes, the less exposure the better," said Jefferson.

"It depends on the type of paint, how old they are, the canvas, all sorts of factors," explained Oscar.

"Factors we can't worry about at the moment," said Anne. "Move now. Figure out what we can salvage from this job once we're back aboard the *Lightning Bug*."

Lars opened the stairway door and held it open for the others who rushed through, Jefferson in the lead, his sack of potential paintings held loosely over his left shoulder. Thickening smoke curled upward through the stairway as they rushed down.

The smoke thickened as he descended taking the wooden steps two at a time. Jefferson passed the fourth-floor landing and continued down. He rounded the bend, took two steps, and something gave under his right foot, which twisted at the ankle. "Whoa! Everyone, stop!" he shouted. Waving his right hand to clear the smoke, he peered down. That wasn't good.

He backed up a step and gasped. Pain stabbed his ankle with each step.

"What's wrong, Jefferson?" Anne said. "What happened?"

"I stepped wrong and hurt my ankle. The steps are collapsing here," he said over his shoulder. "They're old and dry and maybe a bit rotten in places. There's too much smoke to see farther down."

A crash from below punctuated Jefferson's assessment.

"Back up to the fourth floor," called Anne. She turned and led the way.

Jefferson brought up the rear. Each time he took a step pain rippled up his calf. He switched the bag to the other side, which helped a tiny bit, but it was still painful. He hobbled slowly after the rest of the Barnacles, catching up when they paused to assess their situation.

"Well, at least we're one floor lower," Missy said.

"Yes, but dying on the fourth floor isn't much different than dying on the fifth," Oscar said. "We need to find another way down."

"We'd need more rope to climb down from a window, but we can give it a try without," said Lars.

"Maybe you could manage without a rope, but not the rest of us," said Anne. "And definitely not Jefferson," she added. "How's the ankle?"

"Not too bad. I can put weight on it, but it's starting to hurt more. I could go down hand-over-hand with a rope, maybe, but I couldn't grip it with my feet. I'd rather find some other way."

From somewhere above them they heard a crash and then what sounded like furious clucking.

"Is there a fire escape?" asked Missy. "And what was that sound?

"Yes, but would you trust it after what happened at the Triangle Factory in New York?" Jefferson said, answering the first question. "And if the stairs are collapsing, the fire escape probably isn't far behind."

"Good point," Anne said. "I don't imagine Chicago's safety inspections are any better than New York's. What other options do we have?"

More clucking came from what sounded like the fire escape.

"Chickens," Lars said. "Maybe we don't need to climb all the way down outside the building. What if we just went out a window on this floor and used it to get to the third? It would be progress," Lars said.

"Those poor birds," Missy said.

"Keep your mind in the game," said Anne, "We need to get to the second floor. There's an interior stairway there. It connects the ground floor to the second-floor apartments. It doesn't go any higher than that. It's where the lobby used to be back when this building was a bank."

"Right," said Jefferson. "It's in the middle of the building. Maybe the fire hasn't reached it."

"Regardless," said Anne, "we need rope or something we can use as rope. Search the offices on this floor."

As the rest of the team frantically searched around him, Jefferson wrapped his ankle with an abandoned scarf he found on a desk. Then, he tried his hand at opening two small safes Lars and Missy spotted. He couldn't do much running around but at least he could use his talents to provide some welcome loot at the end of this. Presuming they got out of the building.

After five minutes of frantic searching, and a few kicked in doors and smashed open desks, the Barnacles pooled their discoveries: several balls of twine that might support a kitten, but not a person, ribbons that ranged in length from short to very short, and several balls of red wool yarn and knitting needles that might be useful if they had time to knit a rope.

Which, they didn't.

Lars stretched the yarn between his fingers. "It might work if we twist several strands together." He squeezed the ball of yarn in his fingers. "But I don't think there will be enough to get us down. If we were to combine the ribbons and slice the draperies into strips, that might work.

"Will it hold our weight?" asked Jefferson.

"Mine or Missy's," said Lars. "I'm not sure about anyone else. It should stretch before it breaks, though. We'll have a little warning. And it's not that far. We're just climbing down one floor."

"At least the loot is light," Jefferson said, hefting his bag.

Anne glanced around the group, taking them in. She pointed at Lars. "We'll need to go one at a time. Lars first to open a window, secure our rope, such as it is, at the other end, and help the rest of us down. Jefferson, give your load to Missy. She'll go next."

Missy cleared her throat. "I've never done something like this."

"Always a first time," Lars said cheerfully. "I'll help you. It'll be fun. Once you're on the third floor, we'll help Jefferson. Easy as falling off a log. Right Jefferson?"

Jefferson winced at the word 'falling.' Dropping off the side of a building wasn't how he wanted to die, but he couldn't think of an alternative. It was better than burning alive.

"Fun," Missy repeated faintly. "Sure." She squared her shoulders and walked purposely to the window, like an ancient warrior queen preparing to die to defend her people.

"Jefferson, give Missy and Lars the acquisitions."

Jefferson looked at the rope and then at Missy and Lars. It didn't look like it would hold their weight, much less the weight of them and the loot, light as it was. He shook his head. "Ma'am, I think there is a better way."

"Oh?"

"Once they're on the ground, we can use the rope to drop the items down to them."

Anne thought about it for a moment but shook her head. "Too risky."

"And this isn't?"

"Leave everything," suggested Oscar.

"No," Lars said. "I can carry it and help Missy. We didn't come all the way here to leave empty-handed."

Anne looked dubious. Her tongue poked out, moistening her lips.

Lars' face went mulish. "I can do both."

Anne flicked open the curtains and looked down. She shuddered. "Your priority is Missy. Got it?"

He nodded.

"Say it, Lars. I want to hear you. What is your priority?"

He paused long enough that Captain Anne gave him a hard look.

"Missy," he said.

Captain Anne nodded.

"I'll be ok, Captain Anne," Missy said. She smiled, but it was a shaky smile. "I can do this." She took Jefferson's bag with the paintings in it and attached it to her waist with two ribbons. She looked down. Jefferson heard her gasp.

Lars said something in a low comforting voice. Soon the two of them swung out of the window and to the side.

Jefferson hobbled to the window, as did the rest of the Barnacles and stared down the building. Missy's lips were pressed together. Her face looked ashy. The bag swung as if it were a live thing. For a single stomach-churning moment, Jefferson thought Missy would be dragged down by the pendular motion of the bag.

Lars grabbed the rope they'd made and steadied it. Then he pointed.

Their feet scrabbled against the rough brick of the building. Missy gave a little scream, but it couldn't be heard over the cacophony of sirens and the whoosh and crackle of fire.

Lars found his balance first and slid down. Missy followed, as Lars pried open a window on the floor below, sliding down fast and twisting in the air.

Lars caught her as she arrived, but she overbalanced him.

Almost, Missy brought both of them down, but Lars held tight, braced in the window, and pulled Missy through. Her arms went around Lars as he pulled her in.

Jefferson found himself inexplicably jealous. But not jealous enough to want to follow them down the side of a building.

Lars returned, climbing up the side of the building like the cat burglar he was. Graceful, speedy, and quiet. He barely used the rope. Not that it mattered how quiet he was with all the noise coming from the street below.

Anne and Oscar pulled him into the window.

"You're next, Jefferson," Lars said. The bastard wasn't even breathing hard.

Anne nodded. "Get going. We don't know how long we have."

Jefferson checked for the glittering pieces of jewelry he'd managed to stash. Still there. He buttoned his pocket. "What about Missy? You left her on the third floor. I thought the plan was to get us all down to the ground."

Lars screwed up his face looking as if he'd just eaten something sour. "Someone left a cat. She wanted to rescue it."

"And you just left her?" Jefferson tried not to sound accusatory, but he wasn't successful.

Lars gave him a disgusted look. "Wasn't my choice. She ran off after the cat trying to coax it to her. She said she'd find it and head to the fire escape. She's the lightest of us. It should be safe for her."

Captain Anne shook her head. "Damn her. We'll look for her on the ground. Go now Jefferson. And Lars, no more cats."

A loud crack sounded and the building shook. Clouds of dust fell from the ceiling, and Jefferson choked and coughed as Lars pounded his back, which didn't help at all.

"Go!" Anne shouted. "Get Jefferson to the ground. I don't think we have much more time."

Lars laid out their improvised ropes, tying one safety through Jefferson's crotch and around his waist. "Do what I tell you to do. Got it?"

Jefferson nodded.

"And if you're afraid of heights, just don't look down."

"I'm not afraid," he said. But he made a note of not looking down.

Lars looped a short rope between the rope he'd secured on the third floor and a pointy part of building's architecture, a gargoyle or something, Jefferson didn't look too closely. "That will help with the load," he said. "Take a big breath."

Jefferson pulled in a big breath, which was almost immediately knocked out of him when Lars pushed away from the building, slid down the rope, and landed with both feet on the building wall, a story down and near the open third-floor window. More rope trailed down from there to the street below.

"Ever had more fun?"

Jefferson was about to tell Lars where to stick his fun but instead concentrated on maintaining his grip on the rope which stretched alarmingly under his weight. He slid toward Lars who remained braced by the third-floor window, two sacks of possible paintings lashed to his waist.

Something snapped with a loud crack above his head followed by a shout from below "It's them! It's the mad bombers. Kill them!"

Jefferson looked around, searching the crowded street for the bombers. He didn't see anyone who fit that description, but quickly realized that more and more people were pointing at him and Lars. As he slowed his descent, one of the ribbons from their improvised rope fell slowly past him.

Could this day get any worse? If they weren't burned up by the fire or blown up by the mad bomber, they would be torn apart by an angry mob.

He looked up and saw Anne's face briefly before she turned away from the window. How would they ever get her and Oscar down?

Anne reappeared a moment later and shouted. "The rope's starting to unravel. You two head down. We'll find another way."

"Wait" Jefferson shouted, but Anne was already gone.

"No choice," Lars said. "You can't climb back up."

"I don't want to. This place is on fire. But Anne and Oscar are up there."

"They're smart. They'll find a way. Meanwhile, we follow Captain Anne's orders," he said emphasizing her rank. "We'll drop into the crowd, split up, and run. We can rendezvous with the rest of the team later."

"You run. I can't."

Lars looked over at Jefferson's leg. "Sorry. I forgot. I guess we're going to have to brave the crowd." He looked up to the fourth floor. Despite his bravado, he was as worried about Anne and Oscar as he was. How would they escape the flames?

"I saw them leave," Jefferson said. "My guess is to go down the fire escape."

Lars looked down. "Well, we've got no choice. You and me, we need to get to the ground."

"You think they'll really kill us?"

"Crowds. They're dangerous when they're riled."

Jefferson closed his eyes, not wanting to see the angry faces or the ground below. That's when he heard Sapphire yelling at them.

"Damn you! My brother, the stupidest man in all of Chicago. You guys climbing buildings for fun? Burning buildings? While our mother worries. You are going to have your tail whipped but good. And then I'll turn you over to Daddy."

She kept up the patter as the two of them slid toward the ground. Something else snapped above his head as Jefferson landed, and he screamed as his weight shifted to his injured leg. Then, Sapphire punched him in the stomach. Hard. He went down.

The crowd surged forward.

"Oh no you don't," Sapphire said, loudly. "This is my brother and his ratty little friend. No one gets to punish him for this stupid stunt except me. And Daddy, of course. What were you two thinking?"

But either the crowd didn't hear her, or they didn't care. They just wanted to hurt someone. Lars and Jefferson were as good as anyone.

"Hey, we didn't do nothing wrong," Lars said.

"That's right."

One old woman cried out, "Oh yeah? What's in those bags?"

"Er, city planning blueprints."

Sapphire whirled on Jefferson. "You stole Daddy's blueprints?"

"They're thieves!" called man.

"Yeah, thieves not bombers," Lars affirmed.

A handsome man slid up next to Sapphire. "These guys your friends? Actors?"

"Sure," Sapphire said, focusing her baby blues on the handsome man who wrapped an arm around her.

A loud explosion from down the street startled the crowd. Two chickens and a large tabby cat ran from the building and into the street.

"There's another one," someone screamed and pointed.

Missy emerged from the building running after the cat and calling to it. "Here kitty. Here kitty."

"Missy," Jefferson yelled, "let it go. The cat's safe."

Reluctantly, Missy broke off her pursuit and joined Lars and Jefferson. Taking advantage of the confusion, they made their way to the back of the building. There, they found Anne and Oscar coming down the fire escape. It creaked and screeched alarmingly under their weight, but it was apparently built a bit better than those in New York.

"That was close," Anne said. "I don't know if the fire escape could have held much more weight." Looking around, she added "I'm glad everyone made it. Now let's get out of here."

Later that evening on the *Lighting Bug*, Anne bandaged Jefferson's foot while the rest of the crew looked through the loot. There was a smattering of jewelry, mostly junk but a few nice pieces. They'd found one of the paintings for the client. And damned if the rest weren't actually blueprints of the building.

Oscar tapped his fingers on one part of the plan. "You said this was an old bank building?"

"Yeah," said Jefferson. "That's what I learned from my research."

"I think the explosions weren't anarchists at all."

Anne looked at him quizzically. "Oh?"

Jefferson looked at the plans and then he saw exactly what Oscar was talking about. "Captain, the bombs must have been placed here and here." He pointed.

Oscar nodded.

Missy looked puzzled. "Tell me what I'm missing," she said.

"There's a void there," Jefferson said. "Big enough for a good-sized safe. Two or three feet deep maybe.

"Someone wanted something in the main vault on the ground floor, very, very much."

"The bombs were theirs."

"Yes."

"Didn't you say that there was a fortune in that building that was never found?" Missy asked.

Jefferson nodded. "The old vault was emptied when the bank failed—emptied out by the failure, I suppose. There were rumors of another vault, though, a secret vault. Story is the bank manager had a heart attack and died when hundreds of angry customers showed up demanding their money. He was the only one who knew where the secret vault was. Folks looked during the renovation but didn't find it."

"I guess someone found it."

"Maybe not. That third explosion speaks to a lack of certainty." Missy said.

"Could have been us going after that loot," said Lars. "Better than a few rolled up sheets of paper and a bit of jewelry." He pounded his fist on the edge of the *Lightning Bug's* rail.

"Could have," Jefferson agreed.

"We could go back," Oscar suggested.

Anne laughed at the idea. "No. I think I'd rather be floating down the river than bussed up the river to a woman's penitentiary. Don't you?"

They all agreed, but Jefferson noticed each of them staring wistfully at the plans. Perhaps they could return. See what was left. He scrawled a few notes on the plans. It could work. Not today. Not tomorrow. But someday.

HARDLY HUNGOVER IN HANNIBAL

AUTHORS OF LIGHTNING SCARRED
C. S. STEIN
HARDLY HUNGOVER
IN HANNIBAL
A BARNACLES SHORT STORY

Hardly Hungover in Hannibal: *Without exception, this was the most fun we've ever had writing a story. Not only did we get to spend time at a suffragist march in 1913 Hannibal, Missouri, but learned more about one of our favorite characters so far, Sapphire. Carolyn, in particular, feels a kinship with the troubled but joyous Sapphire who is always looking for a bit of pleasure and a lot of freedom. Unfortunately, the pursuit of pleasure can lead to restrictive circumstances. As Sapphire finds out.*

HARDLY HUNGOVER IN HANNIBAL

Sapphire's head pounded in time with the water lapping against the *Lightning Bug*. She'd slept last night bundled tight against the cold air. November in Hannibal, Missouri wasn't the coldest place she'd ever been, but everything was colder on a boat than in a house warmed with a wood stove. For a moment she wished she were still home, still married, still warm, no longer on the run.

But just for a moment. In Newark, she'd been confined like a parrot in a too small cage, hidden from visitors. Now at least she was free. Though her plumage was a bit worse for the wear, she thought.

Above her head, somewhere on deck, Jefferson was explaining something trivial to Lars at an unholy volume. She wished Captain Anne would tell them to shut up. Sapphire felt around her bedding for her flask. Hair of the dog that bit her would be the cure for this.

She looked muzzily at the metal flask engraved with her ex-husband's monogram, the only thing she'd kept after he died and she went on the lam. Too bad she didn't have a lemon, but gin, absinthe, and a dash of hot sauce was just the corpse reviver she needed. She took a swig, felt the alcohol and peppers burn down her throat, smoothed slightly by the absinthe. She fell back to sleep moments later, dreaming of giant hammers crashing over the waves.

She woke later, not sure how long she'd slept. She felt a bit better. Thank God! Or the Devil! Didn't matter. Time to find out what her fellow Barnacles, her partners in crimes both big and small, had in mind for their next score.

When she clambered on deck, Lars and Annie were already gone. Jefferson and Oscar had their heads together working on some mechanical thing. They shushed her when she asked about the plan.

"Go away, Sapphire," Oscar said. "This is a job for men."

If that didn't take the cake. A job for men. How many times was she supposed to hear that? "Shall I tell Annie that?" she snapped.

"Let them be, Sapphire," Missy said, as she walked over to them carrying a bundle of what looked like white cotton bedding with bits of lace peeping out. "You were the one who slept the morning away. Alcohol is the Devil's juice, don't you know. I'd avoid it if I were you. Maybe you wouldn't miss so many meetings."

"You're not me."

Missy seemed to gather herself up, looking far taller than her diminutive 5'2" and towered over Sapphire, despite being half a foot shorter. "Clearly not." She shoved the bundle into Sapphire's arms. "Put those on and get ready to do your stuff. You're the distraction today."

"The distraction? Who am I distracting?"

Missy's sweet smile could have melted butter. "Should have been at the briefing this morning." She laughed. "Get on with you. Dress. You don't have a lot of time. We need to get to the job."

Sapphire grumbled but dropped back down below to dress. When she opened the bundle, she found a cheap white cotton day dress and a purple sash with the words, "Votes for Women" emblazoned on it. The dress smelled freshly laundered. A broad-brimmed straw hat with a purple bow dropped out of the bundle as well. She examined it. The hat was passable, but the dress was too short, shabby, and had a bloodstain on the sleeve near the shoulder. Not something Sapphire wanted to be seen in. Hopefully, no one would take a close look at her. Sapphire added one of her own petticoats and a front-fastening white corset and corset cover before bringing the dress over her head and adjusting it.

When she finished, the effect was demure except for the sash, which declared to one and all that she was one of those women making a fuss in the street.

Sapphire went to the upper deck, holding the sash in her hands as if it were a water snake. "Are you bonkers? I can't wear this."

Missy crossed her arms and glared at her. Sapphire looked away into the waters of the Mississippi. That was a mistake. The lapping waters and slight movement of the boat roiled her queasy stomach. She looked down at the deck and willed it to stop moving.

Missy's words were laced with acid. "You have a problem with votes for women?"

That's right. Missy was a suffragist or some such before she joined the Barnacles on the *Lightning Bug*. Sapphire chose her words carefully, trusting that Missy would understand. "Well, no. But I can't be seen wearing this. People will see me."

"Oh, I see. State by state, we're winning the vote and you're fine with that. But you think it is unseemly to take part. Is that it?"

"Jeez, Missy." Sapphire snapped her gum. Missy could be such a prig. Who uses words like unseemly? "I'm gonna do it. But why do I have to wear the stupid sash? It will make people notice me."

"Because you, Sapphire," she emphasized her name, "are the distraction. What part of distraction are you not understanding? We don't have time for this. Put on the sash and let's go."

At least the sash would cover part of the bloodstain. Sapphire never expected to join the suffragist movement, or really any movement. She wasn't that sort of person. It was just for the day, she told herself. How bad could things get in a day? On the other hand, suffragists weren't known for keeping quiet, which compounded Sapphire's unease. This might not be a quiet afternoon.

There were always reporters at suffrage demonstrations, especially if the women did something dramatic, like blocking streets or chaining themselves to something. They did that a lot in England, she'd heard. Sapphire understood that attracting publicity was the whole point of these events, but she didn't want publicity herself. A photo of her in the papers, especially any of the big newspapers, could be dangerous, perhaps deadly. It could tip her former associates in Newark's mob to her location.

Sapphire needed to be just distracting enough for whatever job the Barnacles were doing, but not so distracting as to focus any photographer's attention on her. She needed to fit in, lose herself among the crowd, and avoid cameras and nosy reporters. Hopefully, there were a lot of suffragists in Hannibal, Missouri. Maybe Huckleberry Finn would show up. He lived in Hannibal, right? That would be a distraction.

Or was he dead? Sapphire couldn't remember.

Sapphire allowed Missy to guide her to the corner of 9th and Lyons Street next to the old Duffy Trowbridge Stove manufacturer, an imposing brick building. It was hot and smelled of sulfur on that corner where row upon row of women, some in the white of suffragists and some in carefully tailored blue serge suits, lined up behind the Missouri Ladies Military Band, seemingly immune to the smell. Sapphire thought they looked like a distaff police force.

Missy practically skipped up to the leader of a group of black women pulling Sapphire along.

"Mrs. Smiley," Missy said in a tone of deep respect Sapphire had never heard from Missy's mouth before. "This is Sapphire. She is your volunteer."

Sapphire took the woman's hand in her own, noting that it was dry and warm despite the cool weather.

"Sapphire," said Missy, "you have the honor of meeting the assistant to Mrs. Victoria Clay Haley, president of the Federated Colored Women's Clubs. She will tell you where the sisters need your demonstration."

"My demonstration?"

Mrs. Smiley gazed at Sapphire with serious intensity for a moment. "My dear, you are courageous. We need more women such as you."

Sapphire quailed. Whenever people started talking about courage, it was certain to be a problem. It almost never meant the person speaking was putting herself in harm's way. "I really am not courageous. Not at all." The words tumbled out of her, one after another after another.

Mrs. Smiley seemed to take her measure. She nodded to herself. "You are afraid. We are all afraid before we do big things. But doing big things opens the heart for even bigger things. It is God's way of preparing us. God cracks us open like a crab to reveal our sweet meat."

An unfortunate analogy, thought Sapphire. She would prefer not to be cracked open. "I'm not sure God is involved with this."

Missy smiled. "I need to get going. Do what Mrs. Smiley tells you to do, Sapphire. All these women," she gestured at the marchers, "are counting on you. Once we're finished, Jefferson will find you. Do what you do best."

"And what's that, Missy?" she asked, not liking the glint in Missy's eye.

"Why, be loud and obnoxious."

"I'm not drunk," she whispered, hoping Mrs. Smiley didn't overhear. "I'm hardly even hungover. Just a slight headache now."

"Then I guess you'll have to figure it out. Got to go!"

Mrs. Smiley directed Sapphire toward the front of the march, where she walked with the rest of the white women, just behind the All-Women's Marching Band and lively tunes they played. Sapphire had no idea women had written so many songs about suffrage. Several had catchy tunes, and it wasn't long before she was singing and dancing along with the rest of the women, enjoying the crisp November morning.

The city of Hannibal looked beautiful in the morning glow. The sun imparted a rose tint to the clapboard houses and brick store fronts. In each of the parks, suffragists and their supporters had set up little tables of refreshments. The air was moist, the trees lush and green.

An older woman who looked soft and happy, like the march was just another excuse for a street party, passed Sapphire a flask and she took a swig, just to be neighborly, of course. It was some sort of strong apple cider, sweet and hot with a just a tingle of a fermented fizz. After that, she felt a bit more kindly toward the suffragists. They weren't all prigs, apparently.

The music and the press of the other women's bodies against her own stirred something in her. Hearing their voices lifted in harmony, singing, it just felt right to be there.

"Votes for Women," Sapphire shouted and felt a frisson of pleasure as the crowd took up her call, echoing back to her as if she were shouting into a canyon. As they marched up the street and past a park, the smell of roses and sweat and the wet November morning dew as it soaked the fallen leaves entered her. It was as close to intimacy as she'd ever experienced in a group.

She almost forgot she was "the distraction" until a woman approached and asked, "Ready?"

Sapphire nodded and let the women draw her to a lamp pole. Another woman snapped manacles closed around her wrists like those used by the police, but different. A swing through design Sapphire had never seen before, they ratcheted down quickly against her wrists, leaving her trapped against the streetlamp's iron pillar.

"Wait!" Sapphire gasped.

But the women started shouting and waving signs. Sapphire's protests, to the extent anyone heard them, were either ignored or considered part of the show.

"Free our sister! Without the vote, women cannot be free."

After a moment of doubt and fear at being locked up, Sapphire embraced the drama of the moment. As she thought about it, this was a lot like acting, and Sapphire was an experienced actress. Well, experienced with actors, which was much the same thing, wasn't it? This could be her role! She joined in the shouts. "Free me! Give me the vote. Votes for women!"

A passing man threw a tomato at her, staining her dress. And then another one. Maybe the old stain on her dress hadn't been blood.

"Stop that!"

Spattered tomato stung her eyes, and Sapphire blinked to clear them. There weren't actually that many men tossing vegetables at her and the passing marchers, but they were making an awful fuss and ruining what was probably Missy's suffrage dress. The march stopped around them for a moment.

One older woman wearing a kerchief pulled out her hatpin and brandished it at them. "Miscreants! Leave her alone."

"Free my sister," another shouted.

And then, as if it someone choreographed it, a chorus of female voices responded, "Votes for women!"

It was then that Sapphire recognized someone in the crowd, a slash of red hair piled on her head, an indecently cut turquoise dress, and enough jewelry wrapped around her neck to tempt any number of thieves. At least those who didn't know who she was.

At first, she couldn't believe it was really Marguerite, but it couldn't be anyone else. Marguerite, Girl Friday to the boss of one of Newark's most notorious crime families. And the biggest blabbermouth east of the Mississippi. Perhaps she could get away before Marguerite recognized her and told the Newark gangs where she was. If not, she didn't like her chances of breathing much after that.

"Hey, let me go," Sapphire said to the woman next to her.

"Let her go!" The woman responded.

"Votes for women!" said the rest of the crowd nearby.

"I mean it, get these cuffs off me," Sapphire said, twisting in the cuffs to make her point.

"Free our sister! Free your mother. Votes for women!"

The fuss drew Marguerite's gaze, who looked amused at the show. Sapphire looked down and away, avoiding Marguerite's eyes. Hopefully, the crowd and the tomato pulp dripping from her hair would conceal her.

Just as Sapphire breathed again, thinking she hadn't been recognized, Marguerite's eyes widened and then she grinned.

Sapphire shuddered with dread. Marguerite had a terrible sense of the humorous. She said something to her companion. If Sapphire were a lip reader, she would have known whether the word Marguerite's lips made was her name. But Sapphire wasn't. Still, it stood to reason that's what it was. She needed to get out of these cuffs and away from here.

She studied them. They weren't at all like the police manacles she'd seen before. Those were much heavier than these and fastened around a straight iron post, almost an inch wide. Darbys, her ex-husband called them. These were much lighter than darbys, particularly the chain connecting the two cuffs.

She twisted around to check. Could she twist the chain and break it? Or perhaps she could pick the lock. She lacked Jefferson's expertise, but the keyhole was small and within reach of her fingers. She'd watched Jefferson hone his skills on padlocks. Perhaps she could force this lock with the right tool. Her hatpin might work. She bent her head and raised her cuffed wrists, but chained as she was around the pole, her fingers couldn't quite reach the hatpin's nub to pull it out.

As Sapphire bent and twisted and contorted, trying to reach the hatpin, a shadow loomed over her.

"Ahem," said a gruff voice.

Sapphire looked up to see a police officer, a local deputy, according to his shiny badge. He was a large man with a slight florid cast to his face. He looked like he'd been drawn out of his breakfast to deal with the suffragists and didn't much like that. He even smelled slightly of ham, eggs, and, inexplicably, cabbage. "Now see here missy, you can't just tie yourself to lamp posts. You're disrupting a public street. I could arrest you for being a public nuisance."

"I'm not Missy." Sapphire said defiantly, then ruined the effect by pleading, "Please don't arrest me."

"Respect women! She's no missy!" shouted a young marcher in a pristine white silk dress and matching hat.

"Votes for women!" the crowd responded. "We're no missies!"

The cop turned to the woman who'd chained Sapphire to the lamppost. She'd remained nearby and stood with a half dozen other women who led the passing marchers in assorted chants. "Unlock her and disperse, ladies," demanded the officer.

"Never!" replied the woman who'd manacled Sapphire and still clutched the key in her white gloved hand.

Sapphire twisted around the pole to face her. "Maybe we should listen to the officer."

The woman shook her head and glared at the officer, whose round cheeks reddened in a worrisome fashion. This was the last thing Sapphire needed. Was he going to have an apoplectic fit? Would he drop dead at her feet? A dead cop at the feet of a suffragist chained to a lamppost was way more of a distraction than the Barnacles needed for whatever the job was. Missy had a lot to answer for. Just as soon as Sapphire reached the

Lightning Bug, she'd let Missy know what she thought of being the distraction.

Thankfully, the policeman just huffed in exasperation. "Now see here. This is not a game." Reaching out a hand, he demanded, "give me the key."

The suffragist who'd chained Sapphire (she was starting to think of her as her jailor) shouted back, "Never! We shall go to jail if we must. The entire world shall know our cause and its manifest justice." She lifted up the manacle key, which Sapphire noticed really was quite small, dropped it in her mouth, and swallowed it dramatically with a ladylike gulp.

When things went bad, Sapphire took comfort from the fact they generally couldn't get much worse. Today's events tested her optimism, such as it was. Every problem had a solution, though, Sapphire reminded herself. She just had to find it.

She smiled weakly at the officer, trying for the big-eyed look that had worked so well with her ex-husband, God rest his infernal soul. "Perhaps you have a key?"

The officer grabbed the manacles' chain, lifted it to the extent her circumstances allowed, examined the manacles, and then harrumphed. "You have earned yourself time in jail, Madame. I do not take kindly to being mocked by your sort. Obviously, these are unique items. I've never seen their like before. Something new, or perhaps something you ladies had made special? Not to worry, though. The chain's thin. I'll get some friends and a saw and cut you from this lamppost. He smiled grimly. "Then, we'll arrest you and the rest of these troublesome women."

With that, he stalked off, swinging his billy club. Sapphire hoped that was just for effect and that he wouldn't actually use it. Him or his promised friends. She didn't want anyone hurt, least of all her.

"Oh God!" Sapphire moaned.

"Don't worry sister! Your courage is an inspiration to us all. Look at how loud the marchers have become. And we shall not let you go to jail alone." Then she burst into a song about how they were all united in jail, which wasn't as comforting to Sapphire as the woman probably intended.

It was while the suffragist was in the third stanza of what was clearly a very long song, perhaps composed in jail by people who had nothing better to do, that things got worse.

Marguerite approached, smelling like Wrigley's Juicy Fruit and whiskey, her hair curled tight to her head. She smiled like a lion scenting a kill. "Hey, Suzy. Figured you were dead."

Sapphire closed her eyes, hoping against hope that Marguerite would be gone by the time she opened them. Maybe the cop would come back and arrest her. But no such luck. When Sapphire opened her eyes, not only was Marguerite still there, chomping on her gum like a cow, but Donald 'Snake Eyes' Frazetti had joined her. He looked from Marguerite to Sapphire and back again before reaching into his jacket. At least neither of them seemed to know that she was going by Sapphire and not Suzy these days. So that was a silver lining, wasn't it?

Snake Eyes pulled out his roscoe and leveled it at Sapphire's stomach. Of course, if she were dead, she wouldn't care which name they used.

"Hey Marguerite! Hey, Snake Eyes. Long time no see, huh?" Sapphire tried to smile at the two of them, but it came out just a bit more tremulous than she'd hoped. Could there be a more degrading way to go than tied to a lamppost with a bunch of wild-eyed, key-swallowing suffragists singing nearby? Jeez!

She could just hear the eulogy, "She died as an excellent distraction."

Marguerite didn't even bother talking, just walked around Sapphire. Then took out the giant wad of gum she'd been chewing and stuck it in Sapphire's hair. Honestly, this could be worse. With all the crushed tomato goo in her hair, the gum probably wouldn't stick too badly. When Marguerite finally spoke, her voice was low, and it was to Snake Eyes. "Whatcha think? Too public? You want to take her somewhere else and off her? Then get back to me and we'll tell Jo Jo."

"Boss is going to want proof of death. Let's just send word. We're on vacation."

"And let Suzy escape?"

"I'm not going anywhere, Marguerite," Sapphire said. "I'm chained to a lamppost." She rattled the manacles against the pole. "You two lovebirds go. Have fun."

"Hey, who are these people?" The key-swallowing suffragist said as the song ended. She seemed to sense something was amiss, but Sapphire and the lamppost blocked her view of Snake Eyes' revolver. "Are you supporters? Do you want a sign?"

Marguerite didn't say a word, just stood there with that shit-eating grin on her face. "There are so many ways to have fun, Suzy."

The suffragist turned to her. "Hey, didn't Mrs. Smiley say your name was Sapphire? Is Suzy your nickname?"

Sapphire sagged forward, her head shaking at the unfairness of this.

That's when the deputy, whose timing up to that point had been terrible, strode up, followed by perhaps twenty of his closest friends. He carried a hacksaw. His friends all had their billy clubs out and gestured far too enthusiastically with them.

The suffragists seemed all too eager, as well. Shouts rang up to defend Sapphire, and women rushed over, forming a growing circle around Sapphire.

Snake Eyes glanced over his shoulder, saw the cops, and returned his revolver to his pocket. He took Marguerite's elbow and guided her away. "Come on. We have her new name and her location. We'll just get on the horn with the boss. Let the Boss's soldiers take care of her."

Marguerite nodded slowly and allowed herself to be pulled into Snake Eyes' orbit, pressing her boobs against him in a too-familiar way for a woman with a steady boyfriend. As they departed, she waved a tiny wave, like an Atlantic City bathing suit contestant.

Sapphire sighed in relief.

That just left the cops who wanted to arrest her. And the suffragists who wanted to keep her chained to a lamppost. The situation was improving. She would live another day.

Sapphire heard three muffled pops, like far away explosions. They sounded like something Oscar and Jefferson might have cooked up.

Right! Diversion! She needed to be a diversion.

"Votes for Women!" she shouted.

"Votes for Women," the crowd echoed.

"No Surrender," shouted the suffragist who'd swallowed the key.

No, Sapphire thought. That was just going to inflame things. "Cops for women," she shouted, not sure what it meant. "We love the police!"

"Votes for Women," the crowd said.

"Come on," Sapphire said to the police surrounding her. "Join us!"

A young cop shook his head. "I support you, but we're on duty."

"And you chained yourself to a lamppost. That's a violation of the public order," said the first cop. "Creating a public nuisance. If you want our support, you shouldn't make trouble for us, the hard-working cops of the sixth district." He sounded put out.

Sapphire felt the honest truth fill her. She reached into it, molded it, and suffused her face and words with the power of it. She stood straight, helped by the lamppost, marveling at how clear-headed she felt. "There is nothing I want to do less than make trouble for the hard-working police of the sixth district. If you release me from this lamppost, I will not fight you. But please don't take us to jail. Join our cause by letting us go free." The words reverberated in Sapphire's chest, fed on her fear, her passion, and her natural abilities as an actress. Or at least as a lover of actors, which was basically the same thing.

The key-eating suffragist said, "Cops for women!"

"What do you think, Sarge?" asked the young officer.

"They're trouble. They should be in jail."

"Oh, come on," shouted another cop. "I don't want to arrest a bunch of women."

"Yeah, my aunt is somewhere in this crowd." The cop who said this rubbernecked looking around as if for his aunt.

As more women gathered around Sapphire, the hubbub grew. Police and suffragists debated both among themselves and with each other, persuading, posturing, and in the case of the cops, sometimes menacing. It was all a huge distraction, probably much larger than Missy planned Sapphire to cause.

As the crowd of women around her deepened, Sapphire saw Jefferson and Missy working their way through the crowd. Missy, in the lead, paused to greet women she knew, apparently introducing Jefferson to them as a friend and supporter. They glad-handed their way toward Sapphire. Much too slowly, in Sapphire's opinion.

Jefferson slipped behind her, patting her gently on the shoulder. It felt good to have someone who cared about her here. Then he slipped down, and all Sapphire heard was a little metallic clicking and Missy talking suffrage intently with her fellow suffragists, distracting everyone from Jefferson's lock-picking efforts. Sapphire did her best to stay quite still. Not a distraction anymore, but the opposite.

Then suddenly her wrists were free. The blood flowed into places the metal had compressed. It hurt like the dickens as all her nerves came back to life. Sapphire bit her lip to distract from the pain. She stayed as quiet as she could as the three of them discretely made their way through the crowd and to the boat. It was a chore. But she managed.

Once there, she gratefully sank to the deck, seated at last. Her calves ached from standing for hours against the lamppost. The manacles left her wrists bruised. And between tomato goo and the gum, her hair was matted and stinking.

But she was home. The day had warmed, but wasn't yet hot, if it ever would be in Hannibal in November. There was a physical bliss in escape, in finding her way out of danger that she treasured. She'd never quite loved the *Lightning Bug* so much as today. It's movement on the river currents, so bothersome this morning, now felt like the rocking embrace of a mother.

"You did a good job, Sapphire," Anne said, handing her a bottle of whiskey and a glass. "Because of the distraction you provided and Jefferson's excellent work, we had enough time to get not just one of the safes, but all three. Good job all around!"

Sapphire held the whiskey, staring into its amber depths. This was how it all started, wasn't it? Too drunk last night and too hungover this morning to object to being the distraction. There was a lesson there somewhere, but Sapphire wasn't sure what it was. Or perhaps she didn't want to know.

"Drink up! We won today. We can all celebrate," Annie said.

But was it a victory? The Newark Mafia knew Sapphire was alive. They knew where she was and knew her new name, at least her first name. They would come after her. And then?

No.

She couldn't dwell on that. She gulped down the shot, letting the liquid smoke burn down her throat and start its work of erasing the day. Not too much booze. Hardly any, in fact. But just enough. She was fine. She just needed to be a bit more careful in the future. That's all. She refilled the glass and raised it high. "To the Barnacles!"

"To the Barnacles!" The voices echoed back, much like the suffragists had echoed at the march. But this was a warmer, cozier feeling. Sapphire thought she liked it better. Marching with the suffragists wasn't as bad as she'd thought it would be, but next time they did a job, someone else could be the distraction. She was done with it.

ABOUT C. S. STEIN

Carolyn Ivy Stein and Stephen Kenneth Stein write fiction together as C. S. Stein.

Carolyn Ivy Stein loves writing stories about time travel, mystery, fantasy, and romance. Her short stories appeared in *WMG's Winter Holiday Spectacular 2021*, JewishFiction.net, and can be found in her collections, *Lightning Scarred and Other Stories* and *Sweet Lifts*. She received nine Honorable Mentions from the Writers of the Future Contest for her fantasy and time travel stories.

Learn more about Carolyn's work at:

http://www.carolynivystein.com

Stephen Stein is a professor of military and naval history at the University of Memphis and teaches strategy at the US Naval War College. He is the author of seven books on history as well numerous articles on maritime and military history, as well as the histories of technology and sexuality.

His books include *Torpedoes to Aviation: Washington Irving Chambers and Technological Innovation in the New Navy, 1876-1913* and *The Sea in World History: Exploration, Travel, and Trade*. His article "The Greely Relief Expedition and the New Navy" won the Rear Admiral Ernest M. Eller Prize, an annual award for the best article on naval history. His upcoming book, *Military Strategy for Writers* demystifies the often arcane field of military strategy. Learn more about Stephen Stein's work at:

https://stvstein.wixsite.com/stevestein/publications

Together Carolyn and Stephen Stein, write short stories as well as a variety of tabletop RPG supplements for GURPS, Call of Cthulhu, Traveller, and TinyDungeon. When not writing, they play board games and tabletop RPGs, and attempt to discover the hidden secrets of New Mexico.

ACKNOWLEDGMENTS

Much thanks to those who helped bring this volume to life! Eva Papier and John D. Payne read it in pieces and offered valuable advice on graphics and text. Dean Wesley Smith read and offered advice on covers and the order of the stories. We are grateful.

Finally, much thanks to our families, who are ever and always in our hearts.

If you liked *Thieves Berth*, you might enjoy other books featuring stories by Carolyn Ivy Stein and Stephen K. Stein.

Lightning Scarred and Other Stories by Carolyn Ivy Stein

Sweet Lifts by Carolyn Ivy Stein

Cold-Blooded Christmas: A Holiday Anthology edited by Kristine Kathryn Rusch

Particular Passages 4: South Wing edited by Sam Knight

Fanatical edited by Nicholas Whitney

Mermaidens edited by Sam Knight

Mistletoe Moments: A Holiday Anthology edited by Kristine Kathryn Rusch

Upcoming

A Bit of Luck edited by Lisa Magnum